THE EXECUTION

"The execution must be almost due," said Tassoran. "This Guardsmaster, Ilnivar, is by reputation a beast. I do not customarily attend executions here, despite the boredom otherwise, for they come so frequently and, quite frankly, I lack the stomach for it. But it is a thing to show new visitors." His smile was crooked.

Roped together at the neck, a half-dozen prisoners in filthy rags were being urged along behind the ghayal toward the center of the square. One prisoner was a girl, as dirty and disheveled as the rest—but fair, saucy-featured, light-skinned, and bare to the waist.

On the far side of the square, several hundred Vezhiturians stood near a raised stand now being mounted, gawking curiously at a male figure, naked save for a silver mask over his head.

"Yon executioner anticipates his work with considerable pleasure, I observe," said the Bowman dryly . . .

WIZARD OF STORMS

by Dave Van Arnam

BELMONT BOOKS • NEW YORK CITY

WIZARD OF STORMS
A BELMONT BOOK—MAY 1970

Published by
Belmont Productions, Inc.
185 Madison Avenue
New York, New York 10016

Printed in the United States of America

Dedication
WIZARD OF STORMS
to Lin Carter,
Wizard of Hollis,
friend past words.

Table of Contents

CHAPTER ONE:

The Beast-Doom Of Vezhitur
(From the *Ninth Scroll of Firanzu*)

"No," said the Bowman, swallowing another draft of ale, "these southern lands with their public executions make my stomach spew. Were it not that my geas has led me to this stretch of seacoast, I would not stay among such barbarians."

He stretched his gigantic frame, then patted his huge belly comfortably. "But they do serve cursed good food and ale in Vezhitur."

"In all the Greater Satrapy of Pelmanore I doubt me you will find better," said Tassoran, and added wryly, "I have spent the last fiftyday wandering this land, and I know. As for public executions, I agree; they are barbarous. Yet consider: who finds himself confronted by Guardsmaster's axe but he who deserves it? Also, there are few better ways of judging a people than by observing them on such occasions; which study I practice for my vocation."

A fat and sullen servingmaid in her fiftieth year came by and filled their stoups with foamy ale; and Tassoran scowled briefly at her unlovely figure.

When she had passed on to the only other occupied table, at the far side of the small tavern, Tassoran continued. "What *was* my vocation, for as I told you, I now await rendezvous with a great master of hidden arts who has taken me into his service to do great deeds!"

Tassoran paused and dourly considered the refilled stoup that sat before him. " 'Tis cursed *strong* ale they serve here, that I should speak of such matters."

The Bowman smiled slightly. "For remaining close-mouthed, there is nothing like a geas. Suggest to your mighty one that he bestow one upon you, and be carefree even as I. . . ."

"Yet even now you speak of your geas; it binds you loosely, does it not?"

"I have a geas," the Bowman stated matter-of-factly. "It will not permit me to travel away from my goal by word or deed, nor will it permit me to say precisely what its purpose is—or how much of it I even understand. Within these loose limits I am free to do as I wish. You may call that freedom if you wish; yet I may say no more about it."

Tassoran studied the large man, and nodded. The Bowman was the tallest man he had ever seen; and if he were not the fattest it was because Tassoran correctly suspected that his great girth indicated not fat but tough strong muscle.

"But from what you say, it would not prevent you from joining me at the execution today, eh?" It was not that Tassoran thirsted for blood; he had simply become bored past his ability to put into words how bored he was.

"Perhaps not," said the Bowman, and he took a draft of ale. "And then again, perhaps it would. I never know. You are a thief by trade, are you not?" he continued, his tone still conversational.

Tassoran blinked, then laughed. "Nay, a master-thief, if you will. With my skills, I could have stolen enough to purchase a castle in, well, a certain land, before my twentythird year. Now, however, I have found another line of work—and if I told you I was now a hero fit for epic tales, you would then know as much of my present and future as I do!"

"The ale has greatly loosened your tongue," observed the Bowman. "It is fortunate for you I am relatively unconcerned with such affairs."

Tassoran grinned. "You and I, we are fortunate. We are honest with each other even though we are yet strangers."

The Bowman shook his head. "You say that because I told you I am called merely the Bowman. Yet I cannot give you nor any man my name, nor could I were we now the best of friends."

"I shall look for the most officious wizard in the New Lands; thus I will find the one who laid your geas on you," Tassoran said, and stood up.

"Come, friend Bowman, let us to the Square of the Ghayal. I shall regale you with tales of the enormities committed by the Guardsmaster here in Vezhitur. And perchance we may even observe him commit one or two more today. I have heard many tales of his cruelty with the axe. . . ."

The Bowman smiled a little thinly, but he shrugged and rose ponderously to his feet. "Perchance some thief today receives his attentions; true, true, that might be interesting! Some braggart from far lands, may be, come up against bad times in Great Pelmanore. . . ."

Tassoran chuckled—but not heartily—as he fetched out a small silver coin and tossed it onto the aged stained tabletop. The Bowman loomed over the coin and peered down at it.

"A consort, of Zetri melt, by its sheen. Have you been stealing from the Lady Tza's—"

The Bowman stopped; Tassoran's face had gone paler by several degrees.

The large man cleared his throat uneasily and continued in a different tone of voice, "Friend Tassoran, let us gather with the barbarians in the square and study local customs. Inns and taverns are illfamed places in which to speak of . . . important matters."

The hot sun of afternoon beat down upon the two men as they stepped out from the tavern into a narrow alley that stank of fish.

At the end of the alley they emerged into a wider street, covered over in the Pelmanorian manner with billowing multitudes of awnings protecting many small shops and market-stands.

To the left they could see the docks of Vezhitur, ships all tightly moored in anticipation of a storm, portended by the day's peculiarly intense heat. Down the awninged street to the right was the Square of the Ghayal.

Now the shops were empty and barred, goods from stands swept off into securely padlocked chests; and the awnings fluttered alone in the street.

"Execution must be almost due," said Tassoran, and they strode through the many-tinted shade. "This Guardsmaster, Ilnivar, is by reputation a beast," he went on from an earlier thought. "I do not customarily attend executions here, despite the boredom otherwise, for they come so frequently one upon the next that, quite frankly, I lack the stomach for it. But it is a thing to show new visitors." His smile was crooked.

"In my land," observed the Bowman, pointedly omitting the customary identification of it, "those who steal are put to useful work, and those who kill are given to the family of the dead to serve them in the place of the murdered one. If my geas permitted, I would slay this Ilnivar and flee this city forever with a light heart. You say you are under the protection of a great one in the lands; why have you done nothing?"

"Do I look like a hero?" said Tassoran. "I have been called one, it is true; yet in point of fact I am as little a hero, as I see it, as any of the unfortunates due for slaughter this day. Still, it has been a weary fiftyday of waiting, to the which I am not so used, and—"

The long awninged street had broadened out into a great square. As the two men reached its edge, a pikeman stepped into their path, brandishing his weapon perfunctorily.

"You may not pass this way into the square," said the pikeman. "The executions are about to begin."

"May we then stand here in the street and observe events unseen?" asked Tassoran.

But the pikeman had turned away; for an uneven flourish of horns sounded over and over in discordant bray, at the near corner of the square.

A horrifying yawning scream came from the corner, and a ghayal-lizard of the R'shar Swamps humped fearsomely into the square, its great arched back carrying a man dressed all in cloth of silver.

"Ilnivar?" asked the Bowman; Tassoran nodded. "And the beast is a ghayal, is it not? Why does the Guardsmaster entrust himself to such a dangerous animal?"

"It is said that Ilnivar controls the ghayal by the sheer force of his mind," said Tassoran. "Which is why the people tolerate the ghayal's presence, for it could devour a half-dozen of them within a minute, were he loose, and slay ten more at the same time. Look now, here come the—Lord Tir'u, what a wench!"

Roped together at the neck, a half-dozen prisoners in filthy rags were being urged along behind the ghayal toward the center of the square.

One prisoner was a girl, as dirty and disheveled as the rest—but fair, saucy-featured, light-skinned, and bare to the waist.

On the far side of the square, several hundred Vezhiturians stood near a raised stand now being mounted, gawking curiously at a male figure naked save for a silver mask over his head.

"Yon executioner anticipates his work with considerable pleasure, I observe," said the Bowman dryly.

Tassoran nodded again. "He is an artisan of butchery, reputed to be Ilnivar's bastard son. Look at the wench, how she stands fearlessly at the foot of the execution-stand!"

"Then she *is* to be slain? Will they tell what her crime is?"

"Slain? Yes, certainly, she will be slain. She is a thief, for I heard this morning all today are thieves only. So, her hands will be axed off, then her feet, then her elbows, knees, shoulders, thighs, and finally her neck; unless at that point she is fed to the ghayal, which is not unlikely. Pelmanorians fear to be eaten by any beast, for they believe—and they may be right—they will be thus reborn in the body of a like beast."

"She seems a saucy lass," mused the Bowman, "and her skin is fairer than I have seen among these southern lands. She could be from my own mountainlands...."

Tassoran looked at the Bowman, and the Bowman looked at Tassoran, and Guardsmaster Ilnivar called out in a deep harsh voice, "Let the executions be carried out upon these vile and worthless thieves, for my ghayal has not fed these three days, and grows hungry!"

The ghayal uttered its terrifying yawning snarl once more, and the populace surged back several steps involuntarily.

Tassoran, watching the silver-clad Guardsmaster, felt movement and heard a twang from beside him—

and a long thick quarrel appeared in the center of Ilnivar's chest!

Many things happened. Several guardsmen with pikes at ready had been facing the Bowman when he nocked his arrow and let fly at the Guardsmaster. These shouted the alarm, pointed their pikes, and began to run toward the Bowman and Tassoran.

The ghayal, freed from Ilnivar's commands, filled the square with its snarl of lizard-rage, and, opening its fearsome jaws, bit the head off the nearest running guardsman. Whereupon, the other guardsmen realized there was no more question of vengeance but only of survival. Frantically they began running from the beast—and half a dozen in their panic headed directly for the street Tassoran and the Bowman stood in. The terrified guards were followed by the ghayal, whose feet moved slowly but whose stride was long.

The desperate populace, singleminded in fear of the marsh-monster's rampage, surged madly backward out of the square; they poured into side-streets, screaming in horror.

The prisoners, with the girl-thief, stood stock-still by the foot of the executioner's platform, unable to move rapidly for the shock, and the rope at their necks, and their obvious inability to guess which way to flee.

Should the ghayal take note of them, they would have no chance for escape, Tassoran knew.

Seconds only had passed.

Now the body of Ilnivar, red blood spurting over gaudy silver, toppled slowly over to the side and hung by one foot in the stirrup, head almost touching the paves of the square.

The ghayal stopped, turned its head, and tried to snap at the body; then, catching sight of other guards fleeing back up the street from which the whole procession had emerged moments earlier, roared once more and began pursuing them.

The Bowman drew and nocked an arrow after slapping Tassoran's back and shouting, "Free the girl, you fool, and bring her back—we'll head for the docks and freedom. May your great one have the power to protect us now!"

And the Bowman loosed a quarrel at the nearest guard running toward them. The guard fell.

Tassoran cursed his loose tongue this day, cursed Zantain for failing rendezvous ... and then he was out into the square, darting toward the huddle of fearful prisoners, while arrows whizzed by him, each one unerringly striking its guard-target.

He reached the girl, severed her neck-rope with his drawn sword, and turned to run back with her toward the Bowman—but then he cursed yet again, turned, and severed the ropes round the necks of the other prisoners, who immediately scattered.

The ghayal was surging away from the square, roaring more hideously than ever; and the silver-red corpse of Ilnivar was still dangling and slapping at its side. Now the square was almost clear of people.

Thief and thief darted back toward the giant figure of the Bowman, who stood calmly, another arrow ready, waiting either their arrival or another target.

Then they were past him and running down the shop-awninged street; but the Bowman, amazingly fleet of foot, was now running easily with them.

"Give me your sword!" shouted the Bowman. "I can cut the awning cords up there—it may slow them down, perhaps blind them long enough to miss us when we turn aside!"

Tassoran pitched his sword hilt-first to the taller man and glanced behind.

A half-dozen guardsmen had gathered at the end of the street, brandishing pikes and shouting; the pursuit was on.

The Bowman hacked at a tarry hemp cord, and awnings began fluttering slowly downward behind them like multicolored blankets to cover the guardsmen who raced after them.

Then they were at the end of the street.

To the right, another street circled back to the Square of the Ghayal. To the left, a narrow street ran only to the towered prison.

In front were two angled streets leading into the dock area, where great ships sat sedately abandoned against the threatening storm, sails furled against the impending fury of the wind.

Behind them the street was filled with the colorful awnings billowing to the ground. Not a guardsman could be seen among the confusion; no one would see which way they had escaped.

They darted along the street angling in front slightly to the right; presently the street bent further to the right, so that the street of awnings was now hidden.

They crossed into another street, and now were running along a dock-street.

To their right a great ship with crimson hull lay rocking slowly in the water. It seemed no time at all till they had clambered aboard along the ropes that bound the vessel to its morrings.

Once on the main deck, the high railings hid them completely from sight of land.

"We took a chance," wheezed Tassoran, not a little upset to find himself so badly out of breath, "coming aboard not knowing if anyone were here."

"We can leave," said the Bowman placidly, hardly straining for breath at all.

Tassoran glowered at him. "There may yet be someone here guarding the vessel against pilferers."

"Then let us find him, if he is," said the Bowman, still with that maddening calm, "and persuade him of our honest intentions."

"No one will be here," said the girl unexpectedly. "When the spell-storm threatens Pelmanorian harbors, no one can be paid to remain on water."

The two men turned to her. Her green-grey eyes flashed saucily at them. "My name is Laishalla. Thanks to you for your kind and gallant rescue," she said, irony in her tone, "but with the spell-storm due in hours you have but postponed doom for me—and assured it for yourselves."

Tassoran bowed mockingly. "Think nothing of it. My great friend here would do it for anyone in like circumstances." He straightened and turned to the Bowman. "We dare not leave the ship, eh?"

The Bowman shook his head. "We are noticeable figures, after all. I think we must take our chances with this storm. Yet," he said puzzledly, looking at the girl, "this ship seems safely moored, and there are many others like it in the harbor. Surely no storm could sweep them all to sea—and if such storms were frequent, who would sail here under such risks?"

The girl shook her head, her bare delightful breasts quivering with the movement. "Unmanned ships are safe, or as safe as in any fierce storm, which is a ship's risk to run, after all. But ships with men aboard have a tendency not to be seen when the spell-storm's passed by. So it has been along the Pelmanore coasts during man's memory."

"And woman's too, eh?" said Tassoran, striving unsuccessfully for wit to dispel the gloom.

"We are alive," said the Bowman.

"Many have been alive," retorted Tassoran, "and most who have are now dead. Spare me philosophy."

"Can you not intercede with your mighty one?" asked the Bowman unruffledly. "Surely such a—"

"He has failed rendezvous, as I told you," said Tassoran. "We must take our chances alone."

The Bowman sighed, although not dispiritedly.

Tassoran's face suddenly brightened. "Your geas! Would it have permitted you this action if it led to certain doom?"

"How should I know?" said the Bowman. "But it is a thought."

"Then let us find the galley," said Laishalla, her face also brightening. "With food in our bellies, at least we needn't face starvation."

Both men turned to the girl, then to each other; then they shrugged and laughed together, and Tassoran took his sword to a battened hatch, and presently they were below-decks.

CHAPTER TWO:

Claws Of The Spell-Storm

As the afternoon wore on and the wind died ominously away, they wandered through the ship, now tense, now relaxed, as they tried to get their bearings. The waves almost ceased rocking the ship, and the sun's sullen heat weighed them down ever more and more.

The girl-thief Laishalla's influence was quickly felt.

Tassoran had wished for Konarr's presence; he himself did not understand ships, while that burly middle-aged Free Captain had sailed Ocean itself, twenty years ago.

When Laishalla discovered the provisions, she began roaming carelessly, selecting what pleased her and casting unwanted or imperfect items aside, until at last a large and savory stew was bubbling on the restoked galley fires. While they awaited the stew they munched comfortingly on a varied salad rich with exotic herbs and spices.

"If you are a thief, you are a cursed fair one," observed the Bowman as at last she ladled out the stew; and the three attacked their meal as if so many ghayals in the marketplace. "And you cook as if trained to palaces."

She hardly bothered to acknowledge the compliment, but spoke with toying mischief in her voice. "I can also read the script in which the ship's log is written," Laishalla said, and laughed at their astonished looks. "You could do no more than glance at it in puzzlement, could you?"

"I can read the common scripts of the lands," said Tassoran, defensively, "both the princely and the ordinary."

"And I," said the Bowman, which secretly surprised Tassoran. "It is party to my geas." Was *his* tone defensive? So it was no honor among his people to be so knowledgeable? Hill-folk were often like that; so ran Tassoran's thoughts, for he had early recognized that the Bowman's accent hearkened of northland mountains.

"Well," said Laishalla, her laughter again cutting through their momentary ill-ease, "this log,—" and she brought it up to the table from the bench beside her,—"tells a most interesting tale, at least for one who loves the sea. For this ship was built and outfitted by one Lord Raganas in the great and independent sea-town Teriathna, which lies on the border between Ank and Oan by the Sea of Cheg. From there the *Ahthrthu* has for the past three years slowly been making its way down from the far north, stopping at every seaport and trade town on the eastern shores of the New Lands, trading constantly and acquiring thereby ever more precious stores of wealth.

"Now: they carried two Spellmasters of Sezain to ensure prosperity; luckily for us not even they can counter a spell-storm, or this ship would not have been awaiting us all empty."

"Spellmasters . . ." Tassoran uttered the one word and fell into a brooding silence.

"We must be wary of traps, then," said the Bowman, spearing a potato with his knife.

"Such as at those great oaken doors bolted shut on

the second deck below the galley here," Laishalla said.

Now the two men paused from their eating, taken up by her words.

"For behind those doors are the finest treasures of this voyage—Lord Raganas' own private share, his profits, sufficiently incomparable goods not to be further traded. Ay, Varana! but it is a rare thieves' paradise we have come upon here, Tassoran! Almost worth casting off the lines! And with a gentle chaunt of breezemotion that I happen to know, we might brave Ocean, the spell-storm, and whatever defensive charms lie upon those oaken doors."

The thump of a pair of boots on the deck above them brought all three to their feet at a moment.

The Bowman's hands strung his bow and nocked an arrow in easy motions. Tassoran fetched out his sword quickly, and held in his other hand the throwing-dagger he cutomarily kept well-hidden. Laishalla—dressed now in a richly gaudy cloth of shimmering colors she had taken a momentary fancy to—reached down between her breasts to clutch a sigil in her left hand, a sigil hanging from a thin silver chain newly at her neck; and her lips moved silently, her quick eyes darting about.

There was a scrabbling at the hatchway down which they had descended an hour ago, and then a voice came from the top of the ladder into the inner glooms of the ship.

"Halloa, Tassoran," came the voice, loud but conversational. "You've had an interesting day's work! Can you keep your jangled nerves soothed enough not to spit me on your sword as I descend?"

Tassoran grinned relief, sheathing his blades as he spoke. " 'Tis my old comrade Konarr. He also serves our great master in those mysterious matters we spoke of." This he addressed to the Bowman, who nodded, silently unstrung his bow, and returned to his stew.

"Nay," called Laishalla, an edge in her voice they had not heard before, "do not descend the ladder."

"Why not?" asked Tassoran, as he too returned to the stew. "I told you he was a close friend of mine, and no treacher."

"It may well be," agreed Laishalla, "but I must erase the small enchauntment I had begun, lest he suffer ... unpleasantness."

And she stood for a moment, her eyes shut, caressing the hidden sigil between her breasts with her left hand while her right hand made strange wrenching gestures in the air.

"There," she said presently, with satisfaction. "S'cht'-urnuth has returned to his mating-fields. Your friend may descend." And she now sat and applied herself calmly to the stew.

"Come along, Konarr," Tassoran called cheerfully, "you'll not be eaten by the demon after all."

"S'cht'urnuth is not a demon," Laishalla said indignantly. "He is a ... a personal friend. Though it is true he is not human. He may not even be a male, but his manner is masculine, whatever his sex. However, he is able to come only seldom, to my call."

Bootsteps down the ladder and on the corridor to the galley; and Free Captain Konarr, once of Kolkorth, entered the small mess hall where the three fugitives sat eating.

"Good," said Konarr, and, sitting down uninvited, immediately helped himself at the stew ladle. "Ser Zantain laid a spell of finding upon me as a last resort, and as a consequence I have not eaten in two days. Damned inconveniences of magic ... however,

I was spared severe pangs of hunger by the strength of the spell. Till now, at least."

And he began devouring the huge platter of food he had quickly built for himself.

Between mouthfuls Tassoran attempted to explain the last few hours since the Bowman loosed his fatal bolt at Ilnivar.

"No, no," said Konarr at last, and pushed his plate away. "I see it clearly already; you need say no more. The wench is fair enough of face. But you have caused grave problems, Tassoran. I feel a storm arising; immediately it is over, we must return inland to the Malaishur city of Viximalshur. Zantain cannot travel further. Some great illness has broken upon him, and—"

"*Illness?* But he is an—" Tassoran broke off before the word 'immortal,' warned by the look on Konarr's face.

But Laishalla studied Tassoran's face and Konarr's, then said, "He is immortal. Old tales speak the name, old tales indeed; lore surrounds that name through history, ten thousand years and more."

The Bowman's face was impassive, but his words were forceful. "Bah, what nonsense."

"Tell us the epic of your geas," Tassoran shot back instantly. "Ser Zantain has faced down the two most formidable figures in all the New Lands—and in the very presence of old captain here and myself!"

"Bah," repeated the Bowman. "Will there never be an end to this magic?"

"As well ask if there shall come an end to every thing," said Laishalla.

"Theology," said the Bowman, and spat on the deck. "How long before this spell-storm breaks? I grow weary of awaiting doom, even with a filled belly."

Konarr was brave, yet his tanned face paled

slightly. "*Spell-Storm?* What evil are you entangled in now, Tassoran, in Zantain's time of need?"

"I must see the sky to know the spell-storm's progress," said Laishalla, and arose.

Each in his own way thoroughly preplexed, the three men rose and followed the girl up onto the main deck.

The sky had darkened, though it was four hours yet till sundown; the wind had picked up, and now blew steadily from Ocean beyond the docks. The wind smelled strangely different, tainted with decay and hot oily muck.

"Spell-storm," muttered Konarr as the smell hit his nostrils. "I was too concerned for your safety, Tassoran, in this day's rousing, to notice it. Faugh, we are in crucial danger. We must leave the ship immediately, or we are all lost!"

As if in comment to his words, the wind picked up in strength—just as a clatter of arall-hoofs rang on the cobbles of the nearby docks; a guard detachment searching. . . .

"You may leave if you wish, lads," said the Bowman, though his age seemed midway between the two others. "I shall take my chances with the spell-storm."

"Yet no one has a chance with a spell-storm," said Konarr; but he did not attempt to leave. "I smelt one once before, when I was but fourteen, and a fellowship of ours was lost, that did not turn back to port. It is a certain—"

"It is a certain death to return to land," said Tassoran, as shouts among the searchers came to their ears. "This ship is moored well, though Laishalla says that with us aboard that signifies less than it might."

Konarr turned to face them, slowly nodding his head. "It is true the vessel is expertly tied fast to the dock. Yet tales I heard as a sailor confirm this girl's words." He sighed. "Let us then stay here till the storm is over. Things will then be in sufficient disarray ashore to permit us safe landing, and we can be on our way and business."

"Still, I wonder how long it will be till the storm strikes," said the Bowman, as the wind became even stronger.

"It is upon us now," said Laishalla, raising her voice as a torrent of rain beat suddenly at them, soaking them before they could turn to go below-decks.

"Is it better that we go below?" asked Tassoran, nervously in spite of himself. "Will we not elsewise be swept overboard here safe in harbor?"

Konarr nodded and they went below.

Soaked and chilled, they entered the great stern-cabin of Lord Raganas of Teriathna, and saw the savage rain beating against the cabin's wide windows of thick ill-made extravagant glass. They could not even see to the next ship, though it was moored but a cable's-length away.

There was an iron brazier in one corner of the cabin, screened to prevent flying sparks. Laishalla brought fire from the galley, and they crowded around the low flames, trying to warm themselves in the chilled air that only minutes earlier had been swelteringly hot.

After some moments at the flame the Bowman cursed, and began roaming the cabin, opening closet doors till he found the extensive personal wardrobe of Lord Raganas.

"Ha!" he grunted with satisfaction, stripped off his wet clothing, toweled himself with a dry shirt, selected a garment, and arranged the great thick crimson cloak about him.

The Bowman's height was so great the cloak did

not even reach his knees; and so great was his girth he could barely make the robe meet in front. But, satisfied to be in dry clothing, he returned to the fire's warmth.

The others one by one followed his example. None of the three others being within a head of the Bowman's height, they could find more to suit them than the Bowman's mere cloak.

Presently they all stood round the brazier again, each now caparisoned like true sealords of Cheg— albeit lords with drunken tailors, for nothing fitted properly. Lord Raganas was obviously short, and broad of stomach.

Tassoran chuckled as Konarr mock-swaggered all swathed in deep blue velvet court-robes; while he found for himself rich cloths of crimson and black, his favorite colors.

Lord Raganas' taste in women was excellent, on the other hand, for Laishalla had no trouble finding garments to fit. She stepped behind a thin curtain that swayed with the increasing rolls of the ship; then reappeared in a pale gold tunic, with arms bare and hose of pale blue from her feet to her hips. Her long golden hair was bound sedately in a pale blue ribbon.

"If I must die," she said, "I wish to do so looking my best, that the gods will not think me careless of this gift of life and beauty I had."

"You are not modest in your speech," blunt Konarr said, "yet, certes, you *are* beautiful." He spoke as one realizing this for the first time; Tassoran and the Bowman found themselves staring coldly at him.

Laishalla did not miss this, and did a graceful pirouette, ending by the brazier. " 'Tis also warm enough and comfortable, and safer to wear than most women's clothes, should I need to swim for my life!"

Tassoran played at shuddering, but his alarm was

real enough. "Now that is a skill I never learned," he said, "for swimming has no place in Kazemi, nor have I ever had need of it since leaving there for the thieves' quarters of the world."

"It would be useless knowledge out there," said the Bowman, pointing at the windows.

Rain was beating ever harder and harder against the glass, and the raging winds had increased to a wailing shriek so fearfully intense as to make each man quail innerly in spite of all his courage.

Each then looked at Laishalla, who seemed unconcerned with weather as she walked about the cabin examining it in greater detail.

The *Ahthrthu* lurched drunkenly about within the small compass permitted it by its seven great mooring-lines; yet Laishalla moved foot-sure on the lurching deck, admiring a string of jewels in this drawer here, studying the voyage-chart on the bulkhead there, and paying no attention whatsoever to the monstrous fury of the storm outside.

Suddenly there came a loud 'twang,' followed immediately by two more. Laishalla was staggered to the deck.

"The lines are parting," shouted Konarr. "We're for it now. Hold onto something—we'll be adrift any moment."

At the mercy of the storm, the *Ahthrthu* danced heavily back and forth in its newer wider compass, held now by only four lines; and moments later there came a double 'twang,' followed in one beat by a sixth, and in another by the seventh and final line.

The ship seemed to leap forward. Tassoran shut his eyes involuntarily, expecting the *Ahthrthu* to ram into another ship or into a dock momentarily. So intense was the rain it presently became hardly possible to tell whether the ship were traveling bow- or stern-first.

Even Konarr's sea-wisdom failed him, and he sank helplessly into one of the huge cushioned chairs attached firmly to the deck.

"We are lost," Konarr whispered; yet they all could hear him, so sharp-keyed were their senses now.

"Nay," said the Bowman. "Perhaps we have merely been found.

Tassoran glared at him, but the Bowman continued calmly, "For if this is what be called a spell-storm, then, certes, there was someone, somewhere, who cast that spell. . . ."

CHAPTER THREE:

To The Hellcoast

As the storm wore on, driving the ship with it into mystery, time seemed to cease; the howling winds sank to a low moan, and the rain softened to a steady beat against the windows.

Three men and a thiefgirl sat in the great chairs of Lord Raganas of Teriathna.

"It seems we are not to die immediately," said Laishalla. "What, then, is this tale of your immortal master, who cannot keep himself from illness nor his comrades from such fates as these?

Tassoran felt secret admiration, for he was sure it was a real interest she expressed; she was not asking in order to conceal her own fears.

"It is rather a simple tale, I suppose," he answered. "Though it did not seem so at the time. Upon an occasion of combat between old captain and myself, one Shagon, the vilest of Spellmasters, desired me as a master-thief to join with his magic wisdom. His purpose was none other than to steal from the eighth Lady Tza in Zetri a mystic talisman, the Sigil of Tron. Its great potential power, said Shagon, in the hands of the ambitious Lady Tza could have disastrous consequences for the entire New Lands, to which I responded—"

"That you would," Konarr interrupted. "At the same

30

time you were making your mistake I was making my own, which was to join with this Zantain to slip away the prize from Shagon and Tza the both of them, whereupon I went alone to Zetri to watch upon the Spellmaster's preparations for the theft."

Tassoran continued the moment Konarr took a breath. "I then was captured in the attempt, despite a mighty spell enforced upon me by this miserable Shagon. The Lady herself cast me down into the pits under the Lesser Palace to await my doom."

"But I came, instead," said Konarr. "I freed the lad and together we stole the Sigil of Tron from the very Ebon Tower itself, braving great monsters of the deep that guarded the Tower's moat. With Zantain we fled the Queen City, closely followed by the Lady Tza and this strange Shagon."

"Who was," said Tassoran, holding up his arms that moment to assure Laishalla's attention, "none other but the Black Magician of Shaiphar Mount— Azeltarem, himself!"

"The Most Feared," whispered Laishalla, and Tassoran felt a thrill course up his spine. He had impressed this wench at last, though it took a Black Magician to do it!

"Spellmasters," muttered the Bowman. "Magicians. Curse them all for meddlers and treachers!"

Now Konarr took Laishalla's attention. He reached in his knapsack and drew out an old dark battered wooden cup.

"We three, Tassoran and I and our immortal, faced the both of them, great Azeltarem and the Lady—in her own lands! Their savage magic batterings were of no avail; whereupon Lord Zantain drew forth the stolen Sigil of Tron from this very cup!" He brandished the cup impressively. "And in a moment of dazzling light, he absorbed the entirety of its mystic nature into his own being—thus at a stroke making shambles of both our towering adversaries' plans for it!"

"Whereupon," said Tassoran, immediately winning back Laishalla's eyes, "Lord Zantain proclaimed himself to us as in truth that immortal Zantain of the ancient cycles of romance. He drew forth his sword called Legend, alloyed of diamond and silver, proclaimed himself First of the new cycle of Five Heroes, and ourselves the Second and Third of the Five; and—"

"And we journeyed away entirely across Senthar to these eastern lands once more, each in his separate path to hinder questing-spells. Here Zantain hoped to acquire the strength and power of other great sigils that abound here, albeit hiddenly. Yet with this mysterious malady of weakening he cannot understand, the importance of our return to him increases steadily." Konarr scowled at Tassoran. "Now more than ever he needs our aid, for he can no longer even walk, though the strength of the Sigil of Tron itself is his to command."

Tassoran had nothing with which to gain back Laishalla's dancing eyes; and she stared as one entranced at the battered cup Konarr now held carelessly in his lap.

"An amusing tale," growled the Bowman. "Would it not break the geas I may not break, I could tell one that could make a girl's heart beat even faster. But well I know that I cannot speak until my task is done, and with this ship-doom come upon me now, that may well be never."

"An' if there be other cycles of existence, as some wise men hold," said Laishalla to him, "your geas may bind you even then. 'Tis pity you may not speak of it, for I think all here would aid you in your task if we but knew it."

Konarr frowned to see the climax of his tale so casually capped. "The most we can do for the moment is to pray for the end of this storm," he said, with no great civility, "that we may wear the ship about as best we can, the three of us, and return to land."

"The four of us," Laishalla stated calmly. "I can steer, reef, and hand with any man who sails."

Tassoran suddenly paled as, for the first time, nausea gripped his stomach with the lurching of the ship; and he moaned involuntarily.

Konarr grinned heartily at his discomfort, till he saw the concern on Laishalla's face. "Lean forward, lad," he said then, gruffly, "and place your head between your knees. It may help." *Then again,* he thought wryly, *it may not; ah, well, no need to tell him that.*

Tassoran leaned over and misery filled his wretched being; though after a time his head slowly cleared.

Presently Laishalla announced that the storm was weakening. "I think the spell that holds it has dissipated."

Tassoran tried to take an interest, as in mere moments the sea grew calm, the wind dropped away entirely, and warm late-day sunlight filled the air.

"What coast is that?" demanded Laishalla of no one, her fair brow wrinkling as she peered from the window. "It answers no description that I know."

"We are adrift!" shouted Konarr suddenly. "To the main deck! We must try to unfurl the ship's sails—we're close to rock and sand!"

"But where *are* we?" demanded Laishalla once more, almost petulantly, as she rose to follow the others out of the cabin.

"For all I know, Pazatar and Armassic," said Konarr, "or any other place. We are where the spell-storm has brought us, and that is bad enough."

Tassoran hauled himself groggily up the ladder. "The point still is *who* brought us here."

"Yes," said the Bowman, above him. "And even more important—*why?*"

As the Bowman and Tassoran reached the main deck, they saw Konarr already in the rigging, and cursing profusely.

"What's the matter, old captain?" Tassoran called up. "Tell us what to do and we'll try to do it."

Konarr shook his head and slid back down to the deck, hands on a rope in a way that made Tassoran wince. "There is nothing to do," he said as his boots slammed the deck. "There are no ties on the sails to keep them furled, and hence I know no way to unfurl them."

The Bowman frowned. "Sails must be tied in a rolled-up position, which these are; and yet you say nothing ties them there?"

Laishalla turned back to them. She had been standing at the railing facing the low forested land beyond the shoals, and wondering about the unfamiliar trees, tall, gnarled, startlingly green.

"It would seem the two Spellmasters were carried for more than to assure good luck, friend Konarr. Doubtless there were no more than a dozen or two ordinary crewmen, then. Wages saved there from the usual several hundred would go far to hire a Spellmaster, especially if offered a share of the profits to boot." She was innerly pleased to have regained her calm enough for such rationality.

"Magic ties for the sails," said Konarr sourly. "By Limnar Utter-Curst himself, but my life is to be a plague of nothing save clerkly cheats upon me, from now on."

Tassoran looked up at the ship's rigging just as, suddenly, the upper third of the mainmast snapped clean off with a loud 'crack' and began toppling slowly over. At the same time, his feet were knocked sharply out from under him and he landed heavily on his back. He shut his eyes in a sudden spasm of nausea.

When he looked round again, all four still lay in a stunned tangle on the deck.

"We are aground," said Konarr, and spat bitterly as he slowly picked himself up.

Laishalla darted quickly to the rail. "We are still drifting. I think we only glanced a rock."

"No matter," said Konarr. "We shall be aground soon enough." He cursed again.

Moments later the great ship shuddered again, and this time they clearly heard the sturdy hull grinding along the bottom.

Slowly the ship ceased to move, stopping at last with its deck canted at an unpleasant angle.

"Sand and rocks; safe enough. Well, at least it's a fair day, what's left of it," Konarr said. "We're not too far from shore to swim it. Shall we make for land?"

"Why?" asked Laishalla. "If we wait, perhaps as the tide runs out it will pull us free, and so give us—"

"Give us what?" asked the Bowman bluntly. "We cannot operate the ship for we have not the magic for it. Unless that demon of yours can do useful labor."

"S'cht'urnuth is *not* a demon," Laishalla said hotly. "And I have only occasional chances at his powers; it is too complicated to explain. Pooh! Do you think I would have stood there docilely in the shadow of that lusting executioner, if I could have had S'cht'urnuth to my aid?"

The Bowman spoke steadily. "I do not know the ways of magic, and demons, and of those who deal with such and their like. I ask, how soon can you call upon this . . . . friend, again?"

"I am not certain," Laishalla answered after a moment, her tone defensive. "Most of the time when I call upon him, he does not come, and there is no use calling on him again for a day. Then too, he came when I called a few hours ago; hence it will be many days."

The Bowman shrugged, said nothing.

Laishalla continued. "We cannot use this ship; but we do not know where we are, and hence cannot judge if we should chance the land. There may be strange beasts ashore, and doubtful paths."

"I have no counsel to offer," said Konarr, somewhat abstractedly.

"Can you not as a seaman look at the sky and tell us where we are?"

Konarr shook his head. "Not till I see Spea, Fash, and Qul tonight can I say with certainty."

"Say with uncertainty, then," said the Bowman, "though you obviously guess and do not wish to speak."

"I do not know," said Konarr stolidly. "But I suspect what once I joked, that we see before us none other than the northwest seacoast of the Old Lands themselves—Pazatar and Armassic!"

"Pazatar and Armassic! Then we are dead men for certain," said Tassoran awedly. "Yet if we stay aboard. . . ."

"He who brought us here will soon send for us, no doubt," said the Bowman, and Laishalla shuddered in spite of herself.

"The Old Lands," she whispered. "Not for ten thousand years has anyone seen them and come safely away."

"Nonsense," said Konarr. "I saw them myself twenty-five years ago; though as I think most likely, my ship was far to the southwest of here, by a thousand leagues at least. Yet here am I, alive, hale, well, and ..."

He looked around at the others, his jaw slowly opened, and slowly, slowly he began shaking his head 'no'....

"I know nothing of Pazatar and Armassic save the names," said the Bowman, "and that they are reputedly ill-omened, and that many doubt they exist now—or ever existed."

"They existed; but little enough more is known," said Laishalla, in a whisper that now seemed to carry an air of defeat.

This alone was sufficient to alarm the three men, each of whom in his own way had been secretly impressed by her range of knowledge, if dubious of her occasional arrogance.

"The Autarchy of Pazatar and the Empire of Armassic," she began in a formal tone that was reassuring in itself, "were lands occupying two rough halves of a mighty continent. This continent, whose name has not survived the millennia, was thickly peopled, rich in history and lore, all at a time when the New Lands were empty save for howling beasts. We are heirs to much of that lore, albeit it is clouded by time and the mysterious fate that fell upon these people."

Laishalla paused and looked round; the three men were following intently. She drew a deep breath and continued.

"For it is said that, ten tousand years ago and more, a nameless doom struck hard and fearfully; and those who did not flee immediately were never heard of again. Those that fled, perhaps a quarter of all those who lived in Pazatar and Armassic, founded the New Lands, and neither they nor their millennial descendants have ever safely visited the Old Lands.

"For the great mages of the first days of the New Lands let it be known that, gathering together in the terrible shadow and aftermath of horror, they had cast back upon the Old Lands a questing-spell. This questing-spell presently returned to them bearing no message of life, but pregnant with evil power absorbed from traveling over the lands of destruction. This evil power so lashed at these men of wisdom that they vowed 'twas not safe ever again to make a questing-spell upon the Old Lands.

"And that was the last sure knowledge of Pazatar and Armassic."

For a time all four stood in silence, thinking on Laishalla's words and seeing the silent brooding forest strangely green beyond quiet waves that broke and hissed upon the sandy beaches.

Tassoran laughed lightly.

"Are we not heroes," he said belligerently to Konarr, slapping him on the shoulder, "leagued with an Immortal, companioned with the fairest girl–thief and the wisest—and befriended with the mightiest Bowman that ever I in my wanderings across the New Lands and back have seen?"

Konarr turned and looked at Tassoran, then at the others. "Brave words," the Free Captain said after a silence. "And in truth, cowardice serves only one's enemy. I have few words, but here are four together, not two or one alone; and this seems good to me."

Konarr clasped Tassoran's sword-hand between his own gnarled hands a moment, then turned to the others. "Shall we then stand together, or alone?"

"Surely we stand together," said the Bowman, stolid

as ever, though another man surely would have shown emotion. "And it seems to me I stand with three good partners. It is well."

Laishalla looked at the three men—sturdy Konarr, bluff and hearty; quick joyous Tassoran; and the tall broad, mighty Bowman, distant, cool, enigmatic ... and solid in danger as a rock.

"Good comrades," she said, her voice low and her eyes cast down, "I have ever thought my fate in life a strange one, and never have I known the start and meaning of it. Yet here, now, in this shadowed land, I know at least one thing—gratitude that I may stand with three such heroes against that which will be. I will not fail you."

The sun was low behind the carpet of low trees in front of them, and the air brought chill.

"Very well," said Tassoran lightly. "Now that we've been aground for a time, my stomach feels better; and what do we do now?"

CHAPTER FOUR:

First Jest

They waited with some hope for the tide to turn. Should chance then free their ship, luck might give them the means to guide it to some other coast.

But when the tide turned, the ship sighed, canted its deck five more degrees, settled, and did not move again.

"Then we must spend the night aboard," said the Bowman calmly, "for I hardly think we will find more comfortable lodgings ashore this evening."

"It is sundown; the inns are full," Laishalla said, but her voice quavered slightly as she looked out over the silent forest. The sun was disappearing behind the tall strange trees; staggering sheets of color were flung across the western sky.

Four decks down they came across a store of hammocks. "If there are no plaguing insects, let us sleep on the main deck," Konarr said. "The air is clean and fresh out under the night sky and triple moons."

Each slept separately; none bothered Laishalla. Nothing had been said; each already knew she was no casual lass of the villages to be tumbled at whim. She was comrade—not common property. She might choose to bestow her body or herself on one of them; *she* might.

They slept separately, and soundly; and when they awoke in the chill of early dawn, each of them found a spearpoint close to his neck, held by ominous tall figures cloaked in a strange brown shimmering cloth.

Tassoran let out a sigh—and the brown figure in front of him prodded him just under the chin with the spearpoint. The young master-thief felt a trickle of warm blood down his neck.

"Up," said the figure.

They rose, were taken to shore on a crude raft, and there confronted their mounts for the journey to come: ghayals.

Ghayals, half again as large as Ilnivar's in Vezhitur. Ghayals, monstrously misshapen, their backs humped two, three, or four times, instead of the familiar single hump. Their fangs were longer, their mouths larger; and the intense look of sheer hatred in their eyes made the four stop in their tracks for a moment, until spears prodded them forward.

Presently they were all mounted, and the band of ten brown figures with their four hungry captives began its trek.

Noon came, and still no food, no drink, no rest; the sun beat oppressively through the bright green shade.

Though the ghayals rode with their deceptive slow leg-motion that covered distance quickly without seeming to, it hardly seemed to stir the air; no refreshing breezes came to lessen the torments of heat and thirst.

It was late afternoon as the small troop entered a pass in a low range of hills, the first feature to break the monotony of the forest. Looking back from the slight elevation, they could see nothing but more bright green forest, and off to the side the broad glimmering Ocean.

Then they passed the crest of the hills, and the pass opened out in a gentle grassy declivity that led the eye forward to the fantastic sight awaiting them.

At several leagues stood a castle, by a great bay of

Ocean. In the bay were ships—thousands of ships! And past the ships, across a wide gap of water, on a cliff-girt island stood another smaller castle, black and forbidding.

"Daur'umur," said a guard, pointing to the larger castle, whose high turrets and massive impregnable walls showed it a fortress proof against any assault. "Fain'umur," the guard continued, pointing to the island castle.

As they neared the larger castle, they saw people strolling on its battlements, and realized the entire structure was several times larger than it had seemed to be, and more distant.

The ships, too; on closer inspection they were a fleet of dead and rotting hulks. Few had more than ragged tatters for sails; many had settled into the shallow mud.

"They're safe from spell-storms *here*," said Konarr, sadness, mockery, and anger all mingled in his voice. One of the guards cuffed him, but without any great rancor.

Inland beyond the castle walls of Daur'umur was gentle rolling farmland with a myriad different crops, bounded on all sides by low hills.

Finally they reached the huge main gates. A great wooden bridge across an almost-dry moat led to the towering doors opening through the immensely thick walls. They crossed and entered Daur'umur.

Inside was no military compound, no warlike structures to go with the forbidding exterior.

Instead, many buildings, of several different styles and sizes, were scattered behind those tremendous walls. Tassoran thought the buildings, seldom more than three stories, were not particularly imaginative. Later came another realization: *As though their build-*

er had conserved his artistic impulses entirely for other matters.

Between the dully palatial buildings were green parklands filled with trees and plants of every kind, covered over almost everywhere with awnings of fantastical design. Many people clad in every sort of dress were strolling under the awnings; no one walked directly in the sun.

Musics filled the air; each building with its own sound of it. It seemed to Tassoran that the musicians alone here must number in the hundreds. But they never found musicians, save but a handful; and these might well have been prisoners.

They rode up to a three-storied palace, surfaced in plain white marble, whose mighty oaken doors swung wide apart as the ghayals halted.

A figure clad in jester's cloths stepped into the doorway above them, at the head of a wide stairway of twenty thick marble steps.

"Welcome," came a high strong voice, cracked with hidden mirth—or madness. "Welcome, and take your ease!"

The spears that had remained pointed at them throughout the long morning and afternoon were lifted away; the brown-clad figures indicated to the four captives that they were to climb off the ghayals.

Slowly they did so; and when they were on the ground, the ghayals turned about sharply with horrible snarls and trundled off, carrying away all their former guards.

"Come, come," said the mad-voiced jester. "Enter the Palace of Feasting and break your hard fast. All is prepared; come, come now, do not hesitate."

Behind them came a great slamming clang and the four turned with nervous starts. The outside main castle gates had swung shut, leaving only a slight cloud of dust in the roadway from the departing ghayals.

"Yes, yes," said the jester impatiently. "You are here, and cannot leave, no more than any of us can. And yet, here is food for you, prepared with care! Will you not come and rest your travel-weary bodies?"

The Bowman grunted and began patiently climbing the steps.

Tassoran shrugged at Konarr. "No need for debate, I see. Our choices are hidden from us while we do not understand. Let us then at least feed ourselves!"

Konarr nodded, and Laishalla; and they climbed the high marble stairs behind the Bowman.

The jester stood bowing as each paseed him, then followed behind them into a great banqueting hall, festooned with strange banners hanging from the ceiling, banners inscribed with heraldic devices Tassoran had never seen.

Along one long wall were tables laden with food and drink of every kind. Hundreds of people, in as many styles of dress, were serving themselves or standing or sitting about eating from their platters and keeping up a general buzz of apparently lively conversation.

"Here—usually—you will find food," said the jester as they stood just inside the entrance. "Food and drink of every kind that can be produced out in the fields beyond the walls. A truly amazing variety, all things considered. And as for quantity—well, you might as well join in with a hearty will! The fact is that only a very small percentage of this magnificent display is poisoned."

Tassoran stared narrowly at the jester. "*Poisoned?* Yet everyone here seems to be eating quite cheerfully."

"Well, and why not?" said the jester as if it were obvious. "Days ofttimes go by before the fatal dishes strike someone."

The Bowman turned from studying the feasting-hall, and placed his huge hands on the jester's frail shoulders. "Hear me, now," he said gently, with cold iron underneath. "What is this about poison? And then, where are we? Why are we here?"

"Ah!" said the jester with mock satisfaction—and he twisted away from the Bowman. "You are a philosopher!"

As the jester stepped back, Konarr stepped forward, grasping him firmly from behind. The jester yipped in surprise.

"Gently, now," said Konarr, his own voice soft. "Explain us this, and tell about the poison. Or . . ."

Konarr did not bother to emphasize his words with any painful tweaks of the jester's arms, which he had twisted round behind the man's back.

The jester looked at each of them in turn. "I can—I dare—say little. Some of the food is poisoned; and some of the poison is slow. Hence it does not the least good to observe what others eat, and take only that for yourselves; for both of you would die later if one of the subtler drugs were present. Hence too we all eat whatever we wish, with a light heart."

"And why is all this so?" Konarr prodded, his voice still soft.

"I dare say no more," whispered the jester. "I carry only the burden of welcome, here. No more, no more, in mercy's name."

"Some of the poison, from your words, acts quickly," said the Bowman. "If so, less chance to die if one eats from another's dish. Let us have this fine gaudy man here partake of several items. Then we—"

"Some of it works slowly," said the jester, but now

his eyes darted back and forth among them. "It is also bad fortune to test for another."

Laishalla said, "Let the jester go, Konarr. If we would have mercy shown to us, we should likewise show it to others."

Konarr shrugged and released the frail form of the jester, who rubbed his shoulders ruefully, then bowed to them. "Perhaps I spoke as one too proud in his position," he said. "*He* is very just, and very nice in his accountings of us."

They followed him to a nearby table and watched as he sampled slices of cold meat, bites of strange salads, sips of wine and water, slabs of thick warm bread; and they filled their own plates accordingly.

For a time the four picked delicately at food, till the examples around them of hearty eating broke through, and they began to eat with some enthusiasm.

"For," said Laishalla, "whatever the purpose of our being brought here, it can hardly have been to slaughter us as we walk in the door. We could have been slain by the brown riders as we slept on the *Ahthrthu*." And she began eating without care.

The jester nodded. "That is the correct attitude."

When they had finished, the jester opened and poured from a flagon. "The choicest in the palaces," he said, and drank. "I toast to you a welcome, and a congratulations for completing your first meal successfully!"

He laughed, shook the bells on his cap, and drank again. "Will you not join me? It is an excellent fair wine, and . . ."

A distant look came into his eyes then and his voice trailed slowly off.

"Qurval?" he said, after a moment, his voice low. "*Qurval*? No, but I have served you, I served you,

Qurval. A weak jest, master—the antidote, I beg you, oh, oh!"

The jester crumpled to the tiled floor and groveled, clutching his stomach. "It cannot be! No, no, the—"

A sudden gasp of breath and a final twitch; and the gaudy figure lay motionless.

Tassoran realized that the man had had ten breaths from the time he had realized the wine was poisoned. *Or was it the wine?* a secret thought leered at him; but he determined to say nothing to alarm Laishalla.

Apart from an occasional sidelong glance, none of the multitudes feasting in the palace reacted to any of this, except for the four newcomers, who stood aghast.

Presently a brownclad figure appeared through a sliding panel in a nearby wall, picked up the crumpled figure, slung it over his shoulder, and returned through the panel, closing it behind him.

"Supper is over," said the Bowman dryly.

Laishalla closed her eyes, Konarr cursed, and Tassoran stood there, his hand clenching helplessly by his side where once he carried sword and dagger.

CHAPTER FIVE:

Blood Day Of The Ancient One

"It has been a foul and full three days since we arrived here," said Tassoran moodily, staring out a window at high clouds.

"We have much yet to learn," said the Bowman calmly. "We have not gained entrance to fully half the buildings within these walls."

"It were better did we take one of these silent citizens and make him talk," Tassoran retorted bitterly. "How can we learn aught useful by walking among these endless corridors, among a people who are as close-mouthed to us as if—"

"As if death threatened them, did they say a word," said the Bowman. "And no doubt they took schooling from the jester's death, a sign we were ... unsafe. I confess I do not understand it."

Laishalla turned from another window, where she had been gazing down into one of the dozens of canopied parks and awninged courtyard walks. "We have learned much," she said sardonically. "Our captor's name is Qurval; this place is cursed; and death stalks these hallways in many guises, playing many sad games with these pitiful folk. The mystery and hidden truth is simply that we're being played upon, much like our wretched fellows."

"*Wretched?*" said Konarr, who had been amusing himself by tying hangman's knots in a length of

48

string. "They enjoy themselves as at a Kolkorth feastivy! They dance, they drink, they game, they eat, they fornicate where it suits them and with whom they please, they—"

"No!" said Laishalla fiercely. "They have tried *me* already and have tasted my answer."

The three men looked at her; she smiled a little smile and moved her left hand slightly where it rested by her left thigh.

In her hand then was a knife whose narrow blade was as long as her hand.

Tassoran blinked. "Wares of Shulda! You are well-traveled, oh wise thiefgirl with hidden stings!"

Laishalla nodded with satisfaction and placed the point of the knife on the floor, pushing downward a moment later as if to drive the blade through the wood. Instead, the blade disappeared and all that remained was the handle, plain and thin, only a trifle longer than the blade.

Now Konarr blinked. "But. . . ."

"You know not Shulda?" asked Laishalla, tucking the thin handle back between her tunic and the outside of her leg. "It lies not far south of Kazemi, a small town filled with proud craftsmen beholden to no man nor land for their protection. They make such artifacts as my small protectress here, and they prosper."

She patted her leg and smiled round at them all.

Tassoran found his face reddening as her smile fell on him; for he realized his eyes had rested overlong on her fair legs. He was quite startled to find she was so unexpectedly well protected. He thought about this, his mind racing, and he wondered if he had really been planning to take her by surprise one night, tumble her, share joy . . . and what of Konarr, and the Bowman? Did they not feel tingles of delight when she was near, even as he did, and keep such feelings to themselves? Of course; yet. . . .

Her eyes danced with hidden laughter. "Would frankness now cause discontent among you?"

"Perhaps," said the Bowman, unexpectedly.

"Then," she said, her eyes still dancing, "I will remain silent."

Tassoran glowered sullenly at the Bowman.

The Bowman stared blandly back. "The wench is fair, and desirable, and possessed of wit; she has us in her hand like tiny birds pecking for seeds. Yet here we are in the midst of peril, the four of us. Is it not better that we forego our peacock strivings? Let us not speak further of these matters; till we can rest easy in our beds, let us not speak of them."

"How poetic," said Tassoran, edgily, testily; for he knew the Bowman's words were sound, little though he liked them in his sudden-burning veins.

"It would be best to concentrate our minds upon our problems," suggested Konarr, catching the Bowman's mood without resentment. "We must not pay heed to your fairness," he added, nodding at Laishalla and smiling (foolishly, as Tassoran thought moodily). "It distracts attention, delightfully but dangerously. Tassoran, will you heed us?"

Tassoran turned away. "I *hear* you," he muttered.

"Hear *me*, then," said Laishalla. "This is my rede and counsel, and my promise. Do not fear, but let us work together in our present danger; and this I say: That by the Lady Oriada I swear to do no injury to any of you. I foreswear now and for all futures, any woman's hurting-games among you."

She looked about, then.

Seeing that none quite knew how to take her words she sighed, smiled, and continued. "If I share joy with one of you when this great testing-time is done, I swear to share joy with the other two. For though I am but a woman I may choose; and there is naught to choose among you, save but among that which is good. And I shall say no more."

A touch of color had appeared on either cheek, and the girl turned back to her window-view of the courtyard beneath the window of their room, which they had chosen with none saying them nay.

The three men looked at each other, each in a considerable confusion none cared to show.

The Bowman cleared his throat at last.

"It is best we begin our day's adventures. Thin edges of time may come to seem important to us, ere we are done with this fair prison."

Konarr too had need to cough and clear his throat before he spoke. "Once more we face the question, whether to go among the people the four of us together, or apart."

"I say apart," Tassoran said, then cleared his throat. " 'Tis possible we seem threatening to them, treading among them together like fated gloomy messengers of doom."

"Possibly," said Laishalla. "Perhaps the time is here to take four private risks, in hope of learning more."

The Bowman nodded. "Staying together we have found nothing."

"Nothing, save that grim death mocks soullessly at all who struggle here to live when life would seem impossible," said Konarr. "And that is warning to us. There is magic here, and a One to wield it; when we find him, we may find the power to deal with him."

"Even as we did before?" said Tassoran. "Then we had ser Zantain close behind."

Konarr nodded. "Courage we have; power we shall gain; those are all the ingredients we need."

"If we dare to join their games of life and death

..." said Laishalla—but then she broke off. "Let us not speak of portents."

The Bowman stood among a crowd of laughing dancers; his face impassive as ever, he watched them as they wove his motionless figure into the fabric of their impromptu carousel.

Eerie musics sparkled and whined in the tense air; and somehow the Bowman knew this was a dance of death.

Round and round him now they madly danced, intent in silence on their figures, feet slapping intricately on the orange paves under pathways of blue awnings and scarlet canopies. A huge torch burned fiercely in a brazier, spewing darkly pleasant-smelling smoke throughout the small courtyard, though it was scarcely noon and insects were not about.

Then he felt the paving-stone beneath his feet shift slightly; with an inarticulate roar he sprang instinctively away, just as the stone dropped downward, out of sight into a noisome pit that stank of decay and seemed to whisper with the hiss of hideous scaley things hidden there among the darkness.

Hands were pummeling on his back now, dozens of them, trying to force him from safety back to the yawning hole.

"A death is called, a death is called," they chanted, fear in their hollow voices as they strove to wrestle the giant figure of the Bowman forward.

Tassoran walked alone down empty corridors.

They had not been in this building before; they had tried, the day before, but the giant doors had swung ponderously shut with a melancholy finality as soon as they neared.

Now he had approached it from the side, through an empty courtyard filled with fountains splashing in the solitude; the door on this courtyard slammed shut as he walked past. Vines grew up the side of the building, twining through grotesque carvings of beasts Tassoran had never seen, nor heard of.

When the moment felt proper, he reached out, tested a vine thick as his arm, found it secure, and scrambled easily up it to the second floor.

A small window was set there, within reach from the vine; he pushed at it.

It swung open with a rusty creaking that echoed through the halls and out into the empty courtyard.

Shuddering unaccountably, he climbed through the window and dropped down to flagstones.

The palace halls were silent as he began carefully walking through them. Open doors along the corridors showed empty rooms, barren even of furniture, a thick layer of fine dust on the floor everywhere indicating that no one had been here in many months.

He regretted his own tracks, but without deeply worrying. He was reasonably certain that his whereabouts were known, no matter what; if not, he had found something worthwhile. And there was nothing to do but to push on and find it; to remain in some tiny way in touch with destiny, by seeking for it. . . .

"Destiny," he whispered aloud, and shuddered again as thin echoes teased at his ears. Thief-instincts tuned, he walked the second floor, and the third.

At the far end of the corridor on the third floor he stopped at last, wondering if there were any point to exploring the ground floor. He stared at the wall before him, trying to force his mind to grow some new thought to work with—and the wall vanished!

Outside, below, was a courtyard filled with people; a smoky torch half-hid the daylit scene.

And, just past an awning, the Bowman struggled against multitudes slowly forcing him toward an ominous pit!

Behind Tassoran there was the scraping sound of steel being drawn from scabbards—many scabbards. He turned his head.

A dozen brownclad figures stood there, swords in hand. One stepped forward.

"You have come where you should not have; you are *ours* to play with now."

The dozen figures moved forward, side by side, filling the corridor from wall to wall. A dozen swords were pointed at as many spots on his body; and onward came the brownclad figures.

Konarr felt dizzy, much the same as at the two times Zantain had prepared him for one of his cursed incantations, chanting moving about, clapping bells rhythmically, all of which made his head spin horribly with trying to think of many things all at a single confused moment.

Perhaps it was the smoke from that torch in the courtyard. From where he stood, having climbed up to look for a moment through an open window on a level with the courtyard floor, all he could see was smoke, and legs thrashing about.

Shouts came confusedly; "A death is called, a death is called."

Ominous, thought Konarr, shrugging, but jumping back down to the passageway and walking on. *But I've got work to do.*

He had found a narrow stairwell leading downward from one of the main halls. There had been a locked door at the bottom, but from Tassoran he had learned several tricks for coping with *that* sort of thing; and presently he was silently moving through dim corridors below the ground, lit by tiny windows high in the walls at outside-ground-level. It was at one of these he had paused momentarily.

The darkness grew deeper; then came stairs leading still farther down. He could see flickering shadows from below; occasional torches; Qurval's people moving about. More cautiously than ever, he made his way slowly down the stairs.

Deep laughter rang in the distance, echoing dully along the corridors.

Konarr looked uneasily back at the stairs he had descended. He was at least three floors below the surface, or so it seemed. He shut his eyes a moment, remembering the caverns and tunnels below the Lesser Palace of the Lady Tza in the Queen City of Zetri, several fiftydays, a continent, and an ocean ago.

He shuddered; and went on.

The laughter came again; were there several voices?

Light in the distance increased; someone had lit or brought more torches.

He hastened along the tunnel, realizing that the walls were no longer of stone but of bare earth, with occasional stone pillars propping up the roof. There was the musty dirt smell, and occasionally a fresher smell when he stumbled against fresh soft piles of dirt fallen away in patches from the wall and ceiling.

He wondered what part of the great castle he was beneath. He wondered if the tunnel were safe. Then he wondered why he was worrying; that was a trait most uncommon to him. Perhaps, he thought it was because he was used to soldiering, not skulking. Well, for that he had no choice, not now.

The corridor bent left slightly, and he paused.

Ahead was a doorway, bright flickering lights in the room behind it hidden only by a thin hanging across the door.

Then the lights were gone.

He moved closer, warily.

He could hear nothing.

Then there was a scuffling sound, a muffled grunt of pain—and a woman's scream.

He blinked, felt movement behind him, started to turn—and something slammed into the side of his head and he felt himself simultaneously thrown against the wall. Another blow, this one on his forehead ... and he felt no more.

Laishalla was frightened.

She stood in absolute darkness, remembering how she had seen a brownclad servant in the Palace of Feasting pass through a panel in the wall, bearing a great tray filled with platters which unwilling guests had picked clean.

A napkin fluttered off behind the tray just as the brown figure disappeared behind the sliding panel. But the napkin fell in the track of the panel, holding it open just a fraction.

She had looked about, seen no one paying attention among those placidly eating, then tested the panel.

Stiffly it slid open, and she darted through, kicking the napkin through with her—instantly regretting that action.

For there was nothing but darkness.

She realized then that she had probably been

tricked, that the fall of the napkin had been no accident.

It was a game.

And, whether she were Sage or Axeman, she could not see the Sarjesa; she could not move.

She reached out, touched the walls, tried to find a control to open the panel again; and found nothing.

There was nothing but to wait there in the darkness for someone to come along whom she might somehow overpower, force to let her out. ..

Then she heard a distant noise to her right.

She began to walk along the narrow corridor.

Almost immediately she missed her footing and began tumbling down a flight of stone steps.

Breathlessly she stopped herself after three or four steps, rose shakily after a moment, and continued resolutely downward.

It seemed to her after a time that she had gone some considerable way down, perhaps the equivalent of two or three stories.

Then she uttered a masculine curse picked up from Konarr, realizing she should have counted the steps. Information was what they needed—where things were, what they were, how to use them ... *no use to worry now*, she thought. *Just get on with it.*

Don't worry! Fine advice! But ... will I ever see dark rainclouds again, looming across the hills of Tharet Cevratta?

She forced her mind into attentiveness from memory, and realized that there was no smell of food; yet this was supposedly a supply-tunnel through which food was brought to the Palace of Feasting!

Twice tricked!, a lance-sharp thought pierced deeply into her pride; almost, then, she decided to return.

But the stairs were at an end, and ... was that a flicker of light in the distance?

There was nothing to do but go forward.

The light ahead wavered but grew brighter—a torch as seen round a bend of the corridor, she presently realized.

She drew her knife.

She was nearing the bend, breathing unsteadily, when the light ahead vanished.

There was a chuckle near her ear.

She froze, knife out and ready, and almost gently a hand was laid on her wrist.

Then the knife was wrenched from her grasp.

She would have screamed—but, from behind her, arms reached out, grasping her; and she needed breath to fight.

It was a short fight, there in the darkness. At the end of it her clothes had been torn from her; and she was being held by at least three men.

Sure she knew what was next, she prepared herself for the tricks that made such attempts unpleasant for a man; for the man always had to take one chance ... she smiled grimly in the darkness, and relaxed.

But the men holding her did not relax. Instead she was shoved forward in the darkness into a large damp room; and she suffered only an occasional covert caress of her smooth flesh.

There was the sound of flint on steel, a glimmer of sparks, a tiny flame, and presently several torches guttered fitfully in their wall brackets. She was in a large cluttered room she had no time to notice.

For an incredibly tall, emaciated old man, with a tiny incongruous goatlike beard at the tip of his chin, sat lounging in a padded camp-chair near one of the torches.

He chuckled, and the sound was compellingly familiar—the warning chuckle moments earlier.

"Qurval, madam," said the gaunt man, and inclined his white-haired head slightly toward her. "Called the Mad, yes. Qurval the Mad. How foolish! For I am the Wizard of Storms!"

He looked round with satisfaction at the room.

Following his glance, Laishalla's eyes then widened. The room was filled with countless varied impliments of torture!

Qurval continued languidly, "They might better call me Qurval the Happy, for I live my days surrounded by such joys that I should rather be envied than insulted. Such insults, of course, mean nothing to one such as I! Why, I laugh at them!"

And he laughed, deep heavy laughter that contrasted incredibly with the figure of weak age he presented; laughter that echoed dismally through corridors leading from the room. . . .

"I laugh at everything, I enjoy everything, and hence they call me the Mad!" He shook his head, mock-rueful. "There was a time when I tried to explain, to demonstrate, to induce in others realizations similar to mine. In my own way, you might even say I attempted to spread joy.

"Now, well; now, of course, I hoard it for myself. Since others are unwilling to join in with the proper spirit, they are excluded. Hah!"

"But why? Why are we here?" Laishalla knew how flat and pointless her questions were, but she had to speak to hold her sanity. "Why are my friends and I kept prisoner? Why are all the others here? What have they—"

"They have life," he interrupted curtly, "and an infinite capacity to entertain me; *almost* infinite. Ah, my dear, that sad 'almost,' which when it strikes leaves me no alternative but to give all their . . . freedom, and begin again after the Game of Ending. . . ."

"But *why?*"

"It amuses me—just as it amuses me now to see you there, shivering in your delightful bareness; just as it amuses me to contemplate the doom that strikes the Bowman, even now as I speak!, *and* that gallant young Tassoran. The pit and the sword, ah, yes; my pit-pretties are hungry, and my brown helpers thirst for someone to toy with on their swordpoints. I will see it all presently, though by now it is over; for I do not fear to tell you I own a delicious spell by which I can observe almost anything I wish to see hereabouts, with trifling limitations that—seeing that sigil you wear between your truly delightful young breasts— you no doubt understand?"

He did not pause for her response but laughed again that loud deep laugh that shuddered through the room and corridors. "They die, my dear, swiftly and directly—more directly than is my wont, but you four are a cheeky lot and I prefer to take no chances. . . ."

She could only discard what was irrevocably gone; and concentrate on what remained. "What . . . what of Konarr?"

"He will be here in a moment or two. I shall kill him myself. There is that in him that makes me think he will make less show of fear at first, oh, at first!"

He threw his head back as if to laugh again, but only chuckled; then: "Dash out the torches!" he ordered, in a low stern voice, and brownclad figures threw them to the dirt where they sputtered out.

In the darkness a hand covered her mouth, while others held her arms and legs. One hand again began wandering her body.

"He is very near," said Qurval, low-voiced. "Presently he will pause at the curtain, and . . ."

Laishalla decided it was the man holding her right leg whose hand was now toying with her breasts. She relaxed her leg still further, felt the remaining hand relax accordingly as its mate enjoyed the resiliant touch of her smooth rounded flesh.

She snapped the leg free and kicked back to the pleasureseeker's groin. He grunted with pain and fell back; she twisted, and aimed another kick; another guard fell away—the one holding her mouth! She took a breath and screamed as loudly as she could, hysterical in the situation's momentary madness.

Then there were other hands holding her; she was captive again.

A torch flared up, casting garish shadows.

Lying in the doorway was Konarr.

His head was covered with blood.

CHAPTER SIX:

The Call Of Death

Tassoran needed no time to study the situation; a dozen drawn swords blocked all but one escape.

He looked back down to the bright awnings splashing blue and scarlet above the courtyard two floors down, found himself distractedly wondering for a moment what had happened to the wall of the building, and launched himself downward full onto a canopy directly above the dozens of struggling figures.

He struck with an impact that left him half-senseless, and which sent seven men sprawling.

The Bowman forced himself back from the edge of the pit once more and reached the center of this new disturbance. Tassoran was struggling to his feet, trying to clear his head and catch his breath after that mighty plunge.

The multitude of colorfully clad fellow prisoners now stepped back, something in awe of two men who would fight on against such stupefying odds. There were perhaps twenty figures ringing the two; and once more they surged forward.

"A death is called," came a shout from above. "*He* demands the call be fulfilled. It matters not how—or we all face his desperate wrath!"

All paused and looked up. The dozen brownclad men stood poised at the vacant edge of the third floor above them, swords raised and pointed forward.

Then at a word they launched themselves full downward even as Tassoran had; but, forewarned, he and the Bowman evaded the suicidal plunges.

Half of the figures landed on bare paves and moved but slightly thereafter, if at all. Tassoran's jump had brought several canopies down.

The other six swordsmen landed on the remaining awnings—and the twenty revelers, with shouts of horror and rage held too long in check, then fell upon the six, heedless of their weapons, dragging them off the gaily colored canopies and pummeling them toward the pit.

Somehow all six got to their feet, forming a ragged circle; but the fifteen revelers now left cared nothing, throwing themselves forward to be inevitably spitted on swords.

Weapons thus immobilized, the brownclad men were forced by the remainder of the unarmed attackers once more toward the pit; and, so swiftly did events move, it was only moments later that the first two plummeted downward among scaley hissing horrors . . . and the yawning pave slid shut.

"A death was called for; and two lives have answered below," panted one of the brown ones. "An end to this brawling; away!"

Tassoran and the Bowman stood side by side, gasping for breath as they watched incredulously. The guards left alive were already hauling away dead guards and revelers, while the revelers were simply drifting off in silence. No one paid heed to the two; no one spoke further.

"Sixteen dead or mortally hurt," breathed Tassoran at last. "Death was called indeed!"

"I fear now for Laishalla and the captain," said the Bowman. "But we are fortunate to be alive ourselves."

"We were to die in sight of each other! It was well planned and cursèd well timed. No doubt this Qurval now knows all that has occurred."

The Bowman shrugged. "I do not know what we can further do. So I suggest we eat, rest, gain back strength, and remain prepared for that which comes. . . ."

"I *do* hope you bear up well under it for quite some time," said Qurval, leaning over Konarr. "It makes the end far more amusing, when you break under the strain and beg for mercy. If you understood that it makes no difference, of course, you might not break. But towards the end I shall amuse myself also with this delightfully spirited wench, in front of your eyes; I fancy that will do you in, eh? Oh, yes, yes!"

Konarr shook his head groggily, and slowly realized his hands were tied behind him. A man in brown sat on his legs facing him, whose eyes glinted with anticipation as he followed every word of his thin, aged master with lustful intensity.

Konarr's head felt damp; looking at the ground beside him, he saw blood. A terrible weakness seemed to fill him, as if he were a cup bearing poison of the spirit. In the corner near one guttering torch he saw Laishalla, crumpled on the dirt floor. She lay by a rack of whips, as if unconscious; but Konarr saw her eyes peering through her lashes in the dim flickering light.

"How ingenious," Konarr said, mustering what sarcasm he could. "We had thought you the great games-player here, and yet you are content to torture me straight off; the Guardsmaster of Vezhitur was more imaginative than you."

Qurval smiled coldly. "It is true I begin to grow

bored with my crop of ... players. They suffer, but they cease to suffer with that flair and determination I prefer. They are ceasing to be afraid of death; and against that awakening force no evil can stand. You are quite right; and I shall ponder whether more may be made of you than—what *is* it?" he broke off testily.

A man in brown had entered, greatly agitated, and now lay prostrate in front of Qurval.

Upon the tall one's words, the figure spoke, voice quavering in fear. "Awesome One, your—the plan has gone awry. The thief has escaped the Doom of Swords, and he has rescued the Bowman! Eight of our number are dead, and nine of the others."

Qurval stood motionless, not even looking downward at the wretched figure, whose face was once more in the dirt now that his speech was finished.

Then, hardly moving, Qurval drew a small, very heavy dagger from his waist and casually dropped it point-down onto the guard's unprotected back. It sank itself effortlessly up to its hilt.

The wretch gave a horribly gurgling gasp, and blood poured chokingly from his mouth; he writhed for a few moments, then grew still.

"Were my hands not tied I would applaud," said Konarr, greatly daring. "Your artistry in destroying the defenseless is most ... instructive."

"Silence," hissed Qurval, his voice low and harsh. "You presume too much upon the strength of your insights. I admire perception, and often reward it; but impertinence may leaven my admiration with particular hatred. I am very reasonable except when I hate; be warned."

Without another word Qurval wheeled and strode from the room, signing to the four brownclad men in the room to follow him.

The door clanged heavily behind them, fluttering its curtain. A key clattered in the lock briefly.

"The knife!" said Konarr urgently. "Hurry, cut my bonds! We must do what we may before he returns from whatever grim mission his insanity has now sent him on!"

Laishalla staggered to her feet and limped over to the dead guard. She wrenched the heavy knife from his back and knelt beside Konarr to slice at the ropes on his wrists.

Freed at last, Konarr lurched to his own feet, but immediately sank dizzily to his knees.

"There are three doors," said Laishalla in low quick tones as Konarr recovered. "I came through that one by the torch, you through the one he left by. Where the third goes, I do not know."

"By what route did you come here?"

"Through a servant's panel in the Palace of Feasting, though I am certain now I was tricked to it."

"Then, which door should we . . ." Konarr struggled up again, leaning against a wall. His voice trailed off as he pondered.

"Does it make a difference which door is which? Certes they are well bolted from the other side."

"The floor is earthen," said Konarr, and pointed to Qurval's dagger lying by his severed bonds. "We can, if granted time, dig our way out."

"Ah, well, and to what purpose?" asked Laishalla, and her tone was suddenly spiritless. "We remain prisoners, no matter what we do. He sees everything, knows everything. It is hopeless!"

Konarr searched the body of the dead guard and rose with a grin on his face. "Another dagger," he said. "We can both work at it. And I suggest we try the third door."

He held out a dagger to Laishalla, who took it listlessly. "I will dig," she said, "but it is useless."

Konarr shook his head. "It will free us from this room—and we are armed now, should any return belatedly to guard us. Come now, to work."

And he knelt down and began digging at the hard dry earth with the point of Qurval's dagger.

Presently she joined him; and though it was hard work, it was not so slow as to outlast any of the torches that smoldered and guttered on the wall; and then there was space to crawl under the door.

CHAPTER SEVEN:

Conversations Of An Immortal

.... Now I, Firanzu your legendteller, once of Mallion, once of the hirelings of the Lady Tza in Zetri, must step forth in my own right.

For it chanced that shortly after the portentious events in the Baragan Hills north of Zetri—it chanced, I say—that I departed the employ of the Lady Tza, whose faithful scribe and counselor in certain ancient texts I had been; all of which, and the manner and reason of my departure, I have set down in another scroll.

You will understand that I needed, then, to find for myself a part of the great world where I might serve another usefully, yet have the time for my own quiet scholarly works.

I then met Zantain.

I had preforce halted a twentyday's journey to the northwest of Vezhitur, in my effort to be far from the realms of the Lady Tza. I arrived in the Malaishur city of Viximalshur entirely impoverished, with only the clothes that I wore, two consorts and three scuts of Zetri melt, and my greatchest full of manuscripts, scrolls, and various other scholarly impedimenta. (To carry this enormous chest I had acquired a kepht, which turned out to be half-wild and hence, of course, a sullen vicious brute; I later slaughtered that kepht with a great deal of satisfaction, as a feast to save myself and a halfdozen others from starvation in the fens of Jurdubir; afterwards, everyone was too full to move, and I related the entire story of my life, in verse, with the high-royal rhyme scheme!)[1]

No matter; this ser Zantain lay at his ill-ease within the same poor hostel I needs must choose, and so we came to meet.

Then, and later, I heard the various portions of that tale I have related in my *Eighth Scroll*.[2] "I shall tell you of these things as a legendteller, oh Firanzu; for it is right that affairs of great import be made known all through and through their nature, save for touching on matters of Deep Magick, which are best known only to a few."

Zantain spoke while as yet he lay in great pain; for the ending of present affairs was blank parchment for the chances of change to ink.

And so he came to tell me of certain events in a tavern in Bephan-town in sight of proud Zetri; and of the stealing of the Sigil of Tron, its manner; and of its outcome hours later in the Baragan Hills not far from the Tomb of Lord Vurda.

So also he told me of the great march afterwards these three heroes endured, all across the New Lands and straight through vast untenanted barbarian Senthar. When they reached the borders of the eastern lands, wherein so many dozens upon dozens of war-

---

[1] Firanzu includes many of these personal verses in his *Scrolls*. I have either omitted them entirely or in the translation reduced them to simple prose. It is not easy to find in English the proliferation of rhymes necessary to make the High-Royal Rhyme of Armassic; and Firanzu becomes tedious when versifying on the dramatic events of his career.

[2] Edited and done into English as THE PLAYERS OF HELL by Dave Van Arnam (in Belmont Double B60-077, with A LAMP FOR MEDUSA by William Tenn).

ring political entities struggle in an area twice or thrice the size of peaceful unified Tarmisorn, they separated. Each thereafter moved through different lands to seaport rendezvous.

"This was needful, for I need more power," ser Zantain said, dropping to a parenthetical tone of voice. "Making our leisurely way, we could hear the countless rumors of the many lands; and when we should come together at Vezhitur and compare our legends, we would know where next to proceed.

"For I will not hide that things have gone strangely with me since the Baragan Hills. My memory is unaccountably dim; my grasp of the flow of things is weak. I know I entertained no such weaknesses in days long past, at the third Tza's court.

"I can no longer do that which I wish to do; when I raise my hand to do some intricate work such as is called magic, I cannot accomplish it cleanly. Things go awry; my words lack force; my mind cannot concentrate upon the energies that move these inner events outward to success."

I listened in utter silence, not daring anything that might hinder the flowing unfolding of an entire new cycle of legend being given to *me* to unfold to the world....

"Now I am being spied upon—and I need your help!"

I did not have time to think on whether it were proper for a scholar and a mere legendteller to walk straight-upright in his own tale while telling of it, and pretending to show himself a hero as bold as the next.

For Zantain spoke on, and told how for several days he lay in a stupor of sleep. The Free Captain had found him and he had cobbled up a sort of finding-spell to help Konarr locate Tassoran; as a consequence he was exhausted past his ability to understand.

But presently he felt stronger, which was fortune or his excellent instincts, for an enemy lay somewhere in Viximalshur, the Dark City of Malaishur—an enemy seeking out his condition and knowledge by hidden ways.

For though fevers and wastings of flesh and spirit had obscured his strength and power, Zantain could still sense a questing-spell drifting near, and note a familiar savor to it.

The Lady Tza herself? No, not so strong, he quickly realized; but now there was a bond between him and his subtle foe.

It needed, then, only to arrange a modest trap—and by this time I was hardly surprised to find myself agreeing to his entreaty—to present myself to this hidden seaker, as being known as privy-scribe unto the Lady for nine years.

I found in a dank sour room (much like mine, and Zantain's) a dour young Spellmaster, his evil aspect not quite hidden by the grey shadows of his cowl; and this one, knowing me, followed quite tamely to my rooms wherein I claimed a potent new device that Tza herself had bid me bring him. . . .

And in my room the Spellmaster found himself clapped about with gyves of iron that sorely mystified his powers and chafed him bitterly, since in his useless fury he was was wasting his source of magic by buffeting fretfully and helplessly against the gyves, which prevented his thumbs from touching each other.

"Your face has a familiar cast to it," said Zantain after the Spellmaster was bound and his grey menacing cowl was thrown back from his close-cropped head.

"No matter," sneered the young-old visage of the grey worker. "Yours too is familiar. You cannot stand long against the Lady, by the pain in your eyes."

"I am of several minds, on what to do with you." Zantain spoke as if the other had remained silent. "First and perhaps safest were to slay you at this moment."

The Spellmaster paled slightly at this. "I carry talismans of safety given by the Lady; nothing may prevail against—"

"Or I could take upon myself a custom of this part of the world, Second, and dismember you joint by joint. Your death would be as certain, but you might thereby be prevailed upon to give me sufficient information to grant you thereafter a more mercifully quick death."

The Spellmaster closed his eyes briefly, then opened them. "Though you have bound me in agonizing fashion, separating me from my powers, you cannot bind my courage," he said, bravely enough. "I will say nothing."

Zantain nodded as if he had planned for the man to say just that. "Then, Third, I have certain powers at my own command which, though they have lately tended to go somewhat awry, may be sufficient to persuade you that you have no alternative but speech. I know, for instance, a fine spell which seizes on the throat of my adversary and makes him speak inner truth no matter what his desires. Of course, it is painful . . ."

Zantain turned away, his own face suddenly drawn with inner pain; then he turned resolutely back to the Spellmaster. "This spell," the wounded Immortal continued, "acts something like . . . thus." He began whispering strange words, touched his own throat, then reached out and touched the Spellmaster's with the same finger.

The Spellmaster threw his head backward with a jerk, and his voice howled like a Sentharu r'luzh, the loathsome corpsedog.

On and on he howled meaninglessly, though Zantain's finger had been immediately withdrawn. On he howled, gasping for breath, until—his face reddened with the strain—he finally collapsed, unconscious.

Zantain turned away, and before I could move he pitched headfirst onto his bead, wherefrom he did not move for a quarter of an hour.

When he rose at last he looked at the unconscious Spellmaster with weary eyes.

"I see the Touch of Speaking is no longer under my control," he said, a trifle of irony in his voice. "Perhaps that alone may be sufficient to persuade this clumsy would-be master of the inner arts that he must speak, for I think that he has no great strength of character. Some destructive ambition works on him, else why did he hire out to the Lady for such menial work as spy on me? He could not hope to harm me; nor had he cause to fear me; some other cause worked here. . . ."

"It seems me," I said, "I heard him named once. He appeared at audience with the Lady Tza shortly after the Festival of High Spring, when she had moved to the Greater Palace. . . . Yes, he was there, amid some dozens of her deepest counselors. I, too, naturally, as her scribe. Now, then, what was his . . . Tamis . . . Kmatis. Yes; Taher Kmatis. He comes, as I understand, from—"

"From Kazemil" said Zantain, and a fierce look of joy came over his worn tired features. "He is the elder brother of my wily young master-thief, Tassoran, and between the two of them is blood sufficiently bad to warrant this Spellmaster's taking on such an unworthy task! I have him now!"

Some minutes later, the Spellmaster Taher Kmatis had come back to consciousness and had regained a trifle of composure.

"Certes, it was painful," he said, but hardly above a whisper, so wracked had his throat been by Zantain's twisted spell. "Yet I expect nothing else but pain, so that—"

"You have somewhat thrown in with the Lady Tza," said Zantain, again as if the other had spoken not a word. "That was foolish of you for more than one reason; but you did so out of hatred for your brother Tassoran, who now safely makes one of my company. And you see where your new loyalty to the Woman of Zetri has deposited you—trapped and bound in the hands of one who is quite willing to prolong your agony for years. For I am older than your new mistress.

"And because of my age I care not how long I must look after your pains, seeing to it that they remain constant, agonizing, striking always in new places. Look you, in lifetimes long as mine, much may be learned about the mere human frame's capacity for suffering."

Zantain paused and observed Taher Kmatis breathe heavily for a time; then, satisfied that his words had had their effect, he continued.

"It happens that I would rather be attending to other matters—though I will tend you as long as needful, never doubt that—and am willing to propose a thing to you."

Though the Spellmaster sought most obviously not to show it, a desperate flicker of interest leaped momentarily into his eyes.

Zantain smiled a cold smile, then sat down stiffly

on the edge of the plain bed, pain clear in every movement.

"Good," he said, after a pause that seemed the effect less of conscious design than of the pain that wracked. "I see in you a man willing to compromise any value—save, perhaps, your veiled ambition and your hatred for Tassoran. Well, then, I shall on certain terms give you your freedom to act once more— toward your ambition and, perforce, your hatred for my young friend."

Now the Spellmaster made no attempt to hide his interest. Breathing deeply, he tried to speak; after a time, he whispered hoarsely, "Your touch on my throat yet burns coldly. No matter; if I may be free, I will hear your bargain and perhaps agree, though the Lady cannot help but find me out in it some day."

Zantain shook his head. "*Your* intent is to bargain. *I* am not bargaining for your wretched life or for your even slightly less worthless information. You shall tell me what you know, and when I am well, and joined with my two stalwarts once more, you shall depart hence freely, free to take whatever action pleases your sickened mind and heart."

The painful whisper at length cut thinly through the silence after Zantain's last words. "How would you know I speak the truth?"

Again that cold smile. "I do not. Nor do you know whether I will truly act by my word as given. Yet I am an Immortal, and when this illness is past, should I discover you have said me false, I shall pursue you through your lifelong travails to bring you pain such as cannot be spoken of. Do you doubt I am capable of *this*?"

"Nay," came the whisper, at length. "Well, my allegiance to the Lady ends when she cannot protect me against her enemies; seeing as I sit here most helplessly, I see no reason not to tell you what little I know."

"Why, then, did the Lady think me worthy of such a special watch as you attempted to put on me?"

"The Lady Tza does not confide in every hireling; still, I am *not* an ordinary hireling, being a Spellmaster already of the Gjili Order, though I am only turned into my thirtieth year. So it is I know of the power of Tron you most unwisely assimilated into yourself. And, on my speaking of this to the Queen, she smiled and told me you would presently rue that rash act."

"Ahhhh. And yet, it seemed but a simple matter to take the power of the Sigil unto me. Though my old lore has come somewhat out of tune with these present days, a simple absorption was—"

"Was most foolish, as proved in its result, which finds you here in your present miserable state," said Taher Kmatis, greatly daring as I thought; for I sat silent in a corner while these great ones flew each at the other with his words.

Zantain nodded and said dryly, "It is hardly surprising to me to find I was in error. Yet in what manner did I err?"

"The absorption was technically correct," said Taher, his ruined voice sardonic. "Though, as you say, I have not your knowledge in these matters, you did the thing properly. Yet, you acted incorrectly none the less." He paused for a deep breath. "Tell me, then, how was it you failed to consider the *goblet*, in which my cursed brother and that fool Captain found the Sigil?"

(Now, I thought, now surely Zantain must rebuke the wretch for his presumption; which only shows foolishness, to predict about Immortals. . . .)

For Zantain nodded. "I had begun to wonder about

that; but our misplaced rendezvous was hasty, and we needed Tassoran sorely. I recollected the goblet not long after Konarr left, but to my mild dismay he had taken the cup with him, so—"

"No matter," said Taher Kmatis, and could not conceal a sneer. "Though you may rue the cup's departure, that is no matter at all, for my own case. Hear this, then: the cup is none other than the Goblet of Tron—and when you absorbed the Sigil's power, you upset a balance held between the two for how many ages I know not. All that I do know is that a bond has grown between these two symbols of power in Tron, since that hidden time before time when Tron himself kept his treasures by him, from his cup quaffing his mighty brew of immortality.

"And now you suffer for disrupting that bond. My purpose here is thus quickly told, for the Lady Tza wished to know the speed and extent of your suffering, whether great enough to sustain action on her part. What action I know not; you must know it is not the way of such as the Lady to confide her plans, even in Spellmasters."

"Of the Gjili Order," Zantain said sardonically. "Think you not I know how many levels lie above you in your path toward power you do not understand?"

Taher Kmatis made an impatient gesture with his hand, as if changing subject manually. "Will you not grant me the boon of telling me in what era you became an Immortal?"

"Do you know the same for the Lady Tza and for Azeltarem the Black?" Zantain responded immediately; while I remained speechless at Taher's endless audacity.

"The Lady may predate the New Lands' founding by somewhat; but she is not as old as Azeltarem. *He* I know to be at least 40,000 years. I admit this sorts not with what little I know of the history of Pazatar and Armassic, but. . . ."

Zantain nodded. "Then I am older than either."

Now Taher was taken aback. "If you are *that* old, you may well be a god. Then, if so—"

Zantain broke in. "No, I am no god." Then he chuckled. "For a god needs worshipers at the least, does he not? And I have none." He scratched his head. "You are a worthless body-louse, fit to be squashed by the first to seek you out. However, your information does fit with such things as I know and suspect; and thus you have fulfilled your part."

"When may I go, then?"

"As I said, when my two friends are by me, and the Goblet of Tron," Zantain said, his face wincing with another spasm. "Which, seeing that I can find no trace of them, may be rather more than a brief time. My powers are turning against me, and I am ever more wracked with those imbalances of power in Tron I so unwisely absorbed."

"I have no desire to help you in your problems," whispered Taher Kmatis. "Still less do I desire to aid my brother, upon whom be the curse of Jkala and the—"

The Spellmaster stopped.

Zantain had said nothing; but merely stared at Taher.

Presently the Spellmaster bent his head forward, avoiding Zantain's eyes. "Nay, I withhold my storehouse of curses; though I have exhausted them all many times before to no great purpose, seeing that my bastard brother yet lives and, for all I know, even joys in living."

"Which is more than you do, eh?" said Zantain. "No matter; speak on."

"I have, as I said, no great desire to help you or my

worthless brother. Still less, however, do I wish to remain here in painful iron while events stumble onward directionlessly. You are in poor condition to act, nor is this scribbling traitor here clerk enough to aid you in any particular measure." (Here he gave me a bitter, disdainful glance.)

"You would aid me, then?" Zaintain's voice was calm, without surprise; and I marveled that he would consider such an offer.

Taher Kmatis looked away, and his eyesight rested blankly upon a small window which opened only onto a bleak tiny courtyard. Beyond it were other low mean buildings of dirty stone, much like the poor inn where Zantain, and I, rested.

He seemed loathe to speak; but finally his chin drooped onto his chest, and in whisper almost too low to be distinguished he said, "Yes. I will take the Binding, of course; you would rightly not credit me otherwise. As a Spellmaster—" and here the weak head rose and pale eyes flashed at Zantain—"I could remain hidden even from an Immortal, given such warning as I have had; hidden for a lifetime at least."

Once more that grim smile of Zantain's, but this time he said nothing.

The brief light died from Taher Kmatis' eyes and he slumped once more.

"Well then. I am privy to a new usage of seldom-smoke, from the Lady," he whispered. "As you know, it can be used successfully for distances up to a league, and great Spellmasters have sometimes increased this to two or more. But now the Lady and I can speak with it across the New Lands; for she craves my information quickly. Hence too, of course, it would perhaps be prudent not to omit contacting her periodically, for a time only, and telling her nothing of further importance.

"Well, then. At any rate this same device can be modified, I think; I then might contact my filth of a brother, wherever he may be—if he has not been slain for filching of a beggar's purse. But this will take me time."

"Time is what I have," said Zantain. "We shall devise phrases together to lull the good Lady, eh?"

"Yes," whispered Taher Kmatis. "For in doubly dealing with such as her I have no skill. She is a most frightening master, an awesome woman. I cross her unwillingly, and only in my grave extremity."

"It will make a noble tale," said I, greatly daring.

Taher Kmatis shot me a glance, but the fire was not in his eye as it had been; and I knew that of *this* man I was not afraid.

And that may have been unwise; but which is certainly another tale than this. . . .

CHAPTER EIGHT:

Holiday Of The Nine Joys

"Children!" came a voice from nowhere, reeking with benevolence; its echoes filled the palaces and courtyards and gentle awninged parks.

"For your delight, Qurval this day proclaims the Holiday Of The Nine Joys. There are those of you who have tasted the pleasures of this period in the past; some, more than once. They can tell of the joys to come. Briefly, for nine days penalties are lifted and the dark games are suspended in their courses. Game-taboos are set aside; all may speak freely. And each day will—but seek out your wise elders, who even now are nodding happily in anticipation of what they know is to come!"

Tassoran looked at the Bowman; the Bowman looked at Tassoran.

"Best we seek out a smiling elder, then," said Tassoran. "For it makes no sense to me at all."

"Nor to me," said the Bowman, "but this may prove fortunate for Laishalla and Konarr. It has been more than an hour since we escaped, and—"

"Ho! Over there, some people—perhaps *now* they'll tell us what this all means."

The two men ran toward the far side of the courtyard. Already over a dozen men and women had collected, talking excitedly among each other, as others too ran up.

"The brownclad ones," someone was saying. "They'll serve us now, help us to what extent they can without compromising Qurval's power."

It was a middle–aged man speaking; he was dressed in a dark green toga of a softly glittering substance, and his face was carelined. "I've lasted long enough to see it seven times, and it's always been worth it. The Wizard of Storms, he doesn't go back on his word, take mine for it. Do what you will, lads, and take whatever the brown ones hand you. It will be naught but joy, naught but joy. No one will die, no poisons, daggers, spiders, uots, no spineplants in your bed, no acids tearing at your throat in what you thought was wine. . . ."

The Bowman turned away; Tassoran followed him, somewhat tardily. It was perhaps too easy to follow the trail such a giant made through any ordinary crowd.

"Why stayed you not? The man is still—"

"He has said enough," the Bowman said. "If he says truth, our lives are safe for nine days, and thus if *they* are alive now they will likely remain alive. At least, for the next nine days. . . ."

"I don't believe this," said Laishalla.

"Shhh," whispered Konarr. "*I* do. Keep quiet, or I'll swat—"

"Nonsense. We're in no danger. For almost an hour we've been skulking through these corridors spying on other corridors just like this one, or just like the ones we came through in the first place—well," she ended, exasperated, "he's let us go, that's all. He did not leave us knives for an earthen cell-floor because he is growing *old*. . . ."

Konarr stopped, rubbed his eyes wearily, and said,

"I do not know. These turmoils are beyond me; it is as though we walked again through the smoke-tunnels of the Lady Tza's Lesser Palace, and. . . ."

"Turn left here, you imbeciles," a familiar voice boomed. "Turn here, and you're free!"

"*Qurval*," Laishalla uttered with a horrified shriek; but she was in control of herself immediately.

"Well, let us turn, then, and be done with it," snarled Konarr, and he took Laishalla's arm and tugged her left through an archway—into another earthwalled tunnel.

A few steps, however, took them to another archway, obviously a servant's exit panel.

The door slid open, and they heard a huge voice—Qurval's—thundering over the roofs. ". . . in anticipation of what they know is to come!"

"So come out, then, you two fools," Qurval's voice said, nearby again and not reaching out through the whole of Daur'umur. "You may search out your friends and learn what is in store for the next nine days. Your lives are safe, for now, and every form of practice toward delight has become permitted—nay, not permitted!"

The voice pealed out with laughter which grew louder, booming through the empty hallways of the duty palace they had just stepped into.

"Not permitted! Oh, no. Most humbly and insistently *requested*; yes!"

The laughter began once more—and was as quickly cut off, leaving dim echoes already fading away into silence beyond ear's reach.

Konarr grinned at Laishalla, and though his grin was a trifle lopsided, almost bemused, it cheered her.

"Well, then," she said, and could not move forward; she was certain she would topple from sudden dizziness had she tried to walk.

"Ahhhh," said Konarr, and nodded just as if he had made a perceptive comment. Then he too lapsed into temporary silence as they tried to absorb their situation.

For the first time since she had been captured in Vezhitur with three of the 'suorzahsh-gems of Arwelzara—widow of the Satrap of Pelmanore himself and regent-Wielder of the Satrap's Lash for his thirteen-year-old son—Laishalla felt herself being swept away by the delirium of relief.

A false delirium, she knew; for their situation was still extremely dangerous. In nine quick days the slow slaughter would begin again.

And certainly Qurval would not long pause to bring his attention back to those who had so casually defied him!

Finally they moved slowly along the hall to its door, and walked, blinking, out into the sunlight. Just to their left three naked figures strained against each other as they lay just inside the archway. Two were men, she noticed, and one a young woman; and it was one of the men in the middle—not the girl.

She grinned and prodded Konarr in the ribs mischievously. "If this is how they begin their nine days of increasing delights, what do you estimate we shall all be doing at the end of that time?"

Konarr, she observed with secret delight, turned rather red in the face after his attention was directed to the three sweating figures.

"Let us search out our comrades quickly," he said, after clearing his throat. "At best we have only nine days; and what right have we to expect our luck is the best?"

Laishalla smiled at him, but followed as he turned and walked swiftly toward their sleeping quarters.

The old man's hair was completely white, but his face was young with laughter on his lips. "I would tell these tales no matter what," he said. "For telling them serves me well. So do not think this Qurval calls forth my words. You could have heard them all along since, had you but asked. The only thing I may not speak of is . . . endings."

"Legendteller," said the Bowman in a low tone to Tassoran. "With the manner of those of the 'D—of my childhood, he will smoke from that huge pipe yonder. If we are properly to understand him, we should join him. In the hills, we would give him gold. Here, I do not know; but perchance he will tell us."

The old man waved loosely at the perhaps twenty men and women who had already gathered, smiling benignly as they listened to the legendteller. "First for the newcomers," he said, and proffered Tassoran the mouthpiece for his gigantic hookah.

Tassoran took it and inhaled slowly but steadily, until he was suddenly racked with spasms of coughing.

The Bowman caught the falling mouthpiece with one hand and inhaled, while pounding Tassoran on the back heartily with his other hand.

"Cursed . . . strong . . . tobacco!" the thief managed to cough out, and the spasms racked him once more.

Then he smiled and stopped coughing.

"There is little you can offer me that I would value greatly, I fear," said the old man to Tassoran and the Bowman, fixing their eyes to his. "When you have time, however, and if you do, why, I should like to hear your own stories, for I gather information while I am here. It is my custom to disperse pure information, when I have it. Who can tell me, then, that I am richer or poorer?"

He extended the mouthpiece to Tassoran again,

having inhaled after the Bowman. Tassoran took it automatically, and this time he did not choke.

"You do use strong tobacco," observed the Bowman after handing the mouthpiece once more to the old man.

"Qurval is generous," the old man said with a thin smile. "Only the best ingredients. It is a point of pride with him, always. Even the poisons and such other confections are pure and single in their action; he fancies this artistic."

"You speak freely enough of him," said Tassoran. "Would these others speak as freely?"

"They know what I tell them is the truth," the old man said. "Few of them know more; they are content to live as best they can in this mad place. For, to be here is an expression of personal misfortune for each of us; and to a considerable extent most of these people understand this. But people react to such realizations in different fashions."

He paused, inhaled from the mouthpiece again, and passed it to Tassoran. "My name is Varnashoth. I am known here as a legendteller. If I were to speak truth—and I feel that I must—I would now admit also that I am a Spellmaster of Sezain."

Tassoran choked on strong smoke once more, and anger. "In league with my cursed brother, are you? Says he's called Kmatis these days, yet despises *me* for being a thief!"

Varnashoth the Eld smiled peacefully. "I care nothing for this young idiot Taher, though it pleases me to speak to him in friendly fashion. He is, however, a Spellmaster even as I, though hardly advanced more than two steps inward; and the brotherhood of Sezain do not prate of each others' affairs to strangers."

"No matter, all this," said the Bowman, and patted

his forehead with a piece of cloth. "We want to understand—"

"All this, I'll warrant," said Varnashoth with some sarcasm. "It would take rather a time, I suspect; Qurval is not a simple man, nor are his ways simple."

"If you are a Spellmaster, it should be easy for you to devise a way out of this place," said Tassoran directly, not caring that an answer would surely be overheard.

"I have not all my powers at my command, here," said Varnashoth gently. "For Qurval is far older than I, and though his powers go increasingly awry of late, almost certainly he is immeasurably stronger than I chance to be at the moment. *He* knows well enough who I am and how unlikely it is he can destroy me; and he knows I am wellnigh helpless. Still, I can see a way into the future, at times; and I am content."

Tassoran felt dizzy, and found himself stretching out at full length on the soft turf of this parklike courtyard; several girls younger than himself giggled, and one jumped up, pulling the other three to their feet. His head swam.

The Bowman too felt lethargy drawing him from his purpose; and the sight of four laughing girls coming toward them served to remind him. "Do I not know you?" he said, and his directness made Varnashoth chuckle.

"It is possible," the old one said. "But I am reft of the basis of my powers, here. If I once knew you, the knowledge is sorely bound in with one or another projects I cannot now follow. Forgive the imprecision of my speech, but I may at least say that I do not know you, nor why you might be here and recognizing me. Certainly you are not part of my basic lifepattern, however, for then I would certainly recognize you."

"Very well," the Bowman continued stolidly, "then why are we all here? I speak practically, not philosophically." He had been misunderstood on that point before; very well, he would make it clearer.

Varnashoth smiled. "Of individual destinies I can say nothing; I do not even fully understand my own any more, and I consider myself passing wise. Collectively you were brought here by Qurval's spell-storms, which you very well know. I know of no way out, but I am content to wait. If you have somehow tweaked Qurval's nose, he will pursue you most ingeniously. You may call that the sum of my wisdom, if you wish. Hence, enjoy yourself for the next few days.

"See, your two friends have arrived; to them also I counsel they enjoy themselves. Qurval does not give his word and rescind it, though he has a nice flair for sidestepping."

The Bowman looked round and saw Konarr and Laishalla not far distant, she with a different tunic and hose than this morning, and Konarr with his head newly swathed in white bandages, a tiny spot of red seeping through.

Konarr nodded at the Bowman, while ruefully, and gently, patting the top of his head. Laishalla sat absorbed in Varnashoth's words.

The Bowman turned back to the old man. "In the meantime, then, we should merely enjoy ourselves?" The tone was meant to be clearly disapproving; the Bowman wanted to act, though his head was beginning to feel dizzy.

"Why, yes, of course! Fatalism is a very mixed virtue, but it has its advantages at times when nothing else seems likely to serve. Certainly a hillman of The 'Derh should understand such an attitude."

"Then you know me, after all," said the Bowman.

"You pursue me closely, but you fail to catch me,"

said Varnashoth. "You are obviously from The 'Derh;
I need not know you personally to tell you that."

The Bowman shrugged. "Then you continue to
proffer us no more moral a course than to enjoy
ourselves?"

"Do you understand anything of the true purpose
of what you think of as moral conduct?" said Varnashoth.

"Am not a philosopher," said the Bowman, re-
treating to his stolidity while his head seemed to grow
lighter and lighter. "I drink and I wench and I fight
and I listen to liars who use harsh tobacco in—"

Varnashoth held up his hand and the Bowman
stopped talking. "I am sure you are no serveling of
mine," the old man said, "for I would have enjoined
you to far more silence than is your obvious custom."

This made the Bowman blink and fall silent indeed.

"I can tell this of Qurval," Varnashoth said after a
pause, without further prelude. "He is of these old
lands, yea, and was a great and terrible wise one of
Pazatar and Armassic; for at times he served the
Empire, and at other times the Autarchy, and at all
times himself, for he grew early mad with power.
And I think it is this last which shows itself now in his
weakening; wrong too young, he did not see deeply
enough to touch those wellsprings that *never* weaken
. . . but no matter."

Here the Bowman began no longer grasping exactly
what the whitehaired one was saying.

"Here at Qurval's bidding," Varnashoth droned on,
"you serve him by suffering, as picturesquely as he
can contrive, and he contrives well. From time to
time he calls a holiday from death, as now; if, however, you remain watchful even while you take the licit
pleasures proffered you . . ."

Tassoran had long since lost complete track; had begun to feel he was experiencing later events in between words as they were spoken. And then too, the girl was pressed against him even before he realized it; in fact, she had been there some time.

He grinned. She had nothing on, and she was fair of skin and hair; and Tassoran thought for one long slow moment that it was Laishalla, while fumes bemused his mind and tender happiness suffused him.

Then he realized it was not Laishalla; but the girl was fair, and hotly pressed against him, and nowhere on her were any garments.

Was that Laishalla embracing Konarr? the one last coherent thought stung through him. Then he shrugged as if he were the Bowman, and embraced the girl lustily.

The Bowman felt almost cheerful. Something was wrong with all this, of course; but then, something was always going wrong in his life, else why was he here in this madman's castle?

There were three of four girls beside him now; and with charming gestures they had taken off their scant clothes.

So there he was; and he tried to worry that he was surrounded by bait for a trap that obviously existed, but which he could not see.

Finally, he realized he didn't really care.

He leaned back onto the turf to savor this new thought, and the girls threw themselves over him with girlish giggles.

He wondered why he did not feel uncomfortable; but slowly he began to realize and to believe that finally his geas was not going to speak up, deny him the fruits of this most pleasant garden. . . .

It seemed in the distance he saw Tassoran with
some fair-haired lass; but of course that did not bother him. And then too it seemed he saw Laishalla with
Konarr, and to his dim surprise *that* did not bother
him.

And then he laughed and reached for the girl with
the fairest skin and lightest hair and kissed her soundly, and began caressing her; and after the other girls
joined in here and there, he began forgetting that he
ever had anything to worry about....

Laishalla saw Tassoran and the Bowman, and the
eager girls that hovered near them; and she smiled
tenderly, and she kissed Konarr again, and wondered
about the ritual tobacco they'd all shared minutes
earlier; and wondered about Varnashoth's strange his-
tories and warnings; and she was glad she was with
Konarr now; and what would happen would happen;
and young Tassoran would smile one day soon; and
the Bowman, dourer than Konarr, he too would smile,
and laugh together with her on sweet grass, and there
were eight more days.

CHAPTER NINE:

The Five Cities Of Narzunor

There was a girl, fair of hair; the Bowman wanted to find her. And she had fair skin. . . .

For three days Daur'umur had reeled under onslaughts of pleasure, sweeping all before it. The Bowman lost track of time after several hours; so that he could never say of a certainty what had happened when, but had to partly guess the days.

"Qurval's storms," Varnashoth had said at one point; this he knew for he had at that moment spilled some tart wine on a girl's leg; "have brought none but ye four, in five fiftydays. Ships of late do not so frequently come to his call."

The Bowman laughed rather unsteadily, for his head swam mightily; and he toweled clumsily at the fair girl's leg.

He knew what they had been smoking as 'nklari, it and a milder tobacco than Varnashoth's having come into The 'Derh less than two fiftyyears ago. It was pleasant enough, but it had unloosed the morrings of his thoughts so that things did not quickly separate themselves and become independently meaningful.

As he rubbed the girl's leg, fair pigment came away, revealing skin that glowed with as deep a tan as his own; he being seldom indoors of his own choosing. He thought the skin an illusion of the 'nklari, and had presently gone back to kissing her. And then after that they fell to sharing love again—he could never remember how many times, afterwards, and this he laughingly regretted.

But: *Five fiftydays is time enough for all to grow pale of skin*, thought the Bowman at some point much later, and with another girl.

It was on the third day of the Holiday Of The Nine Joys that the Bowman came round to deciding in his leisurely new way of thinking that he had never seen anyone else here who had tanned skin.

Qurval's brown-cowled servants lived in passageways; when their faces were glimpsed they were pale as cave-fish. And none of Qurval's unwilling guests spent time in the sun, even when they were in the courtyards and parks; but kept to the awnings and canopies. It was as if they did not really wish to be reminded that the sun actually shone freely down upon them as well as on the happy rest of the world.

On the fourth day the Bowman roused himself, declined a morning pipe and did not reach for the too-sweet candy, and with a muddled word of warning to the others, who hardly heard anything he said, he set off to find the girl with the tanned legs.

It had done little good to forego Qurval's amenities, for he was hardly more able to concentrate now than he had the past three days; or were they three fiftydays? He could not tell; nor, half the time, could he remember what he was trying to do.

But he made his way slowly through the great chambers and smaller rooms of the palace in which they had found sleeping-quarters.

And when he had finished, after many times interrupting men and women in various private matters without anyone taking offense (for the fumes of 'nklari were everywhere), he went to the next palace and began again there.

And then at last he caught sight of her, a glimpse as she and a man slipped through a closing door at the far side of a large room whose occupants were in the advanced stages of orgy. The odor of flesh, perspiration, smoke, and aphrodisiac incense hit first; then there were cushions everywhere on the polished floor, cushions covered with naked men and women.

The Bowman chuckled as he made his cautious way with careful footwork through the bodies. Only when he reached the far side and found a door did he recollect what he had come for; he opened it carefully, but the next room held only one old man, snoring loudly.

There was an open archway beyond the old man's room; and the Bowman moved forward.

His head felt ballonlike, though his mind seemed clear. He no longer knew where he was. He did not know where he was going. Halls, arches, corridors, rooms with tangled multitudes all smeared together in his mind—coming into focus only as he occasionally came in sight of the girl once again—until at last and to his utter surprise (for he had once more completely forgotten what he was doing) he came across her only a dozen feet down a corridor far underground.

She opened and went through a door without seeing him, and he was there immediately. He could not open it for a moment, and then suddenly it was open.

There was only a tiny closet space beyond.

And it was empty.

The Bowman stepped quickly inside and shut the door; then he began tapping softly at each wall.

He frowned, tapped the floor, frowned again.

Then he smiled, reached up just over his head, tapped the ceiling, and grinned.

He pushed on the ceiling and it gave at one side. . . .

Now he had climbed up into a damp earthy tunnel; there was only one direction in which to go, which was fortunate since he had again forgotten what he was doing.

It was a long walk, but he kept going because he had decided he had been geased here and could do nothing else but walk . . . and then finally it was over.

He stepped out into cool fresh air that chilled him, sweat-soaked as he was. He was beyond the low hills surrounding Qurval's lands, though he did not then remember that.

It was pleasant here; and he wondered *why* he was standing here until the blow fell on the top of his head.

"We relax our discipline here considerably during times such as the Holiday Of The Nine Joys, good Bowman; but not so much as that."

The man was bald and middle–aged and was dressed in cool white flowing robes, and the Bowman could not believe the way in which he was willing to talk on and on.

They were the Arzun, the Free Men in the ancient tongue of Pazatar.

They knew he was the Bowman, knew of Konarr, Tassoran, Laishalla; indeed, they knew all who dwelt with Qurval in his manic corridors.

And they were free of Qurval.

"Then too," said the Bowman, who had waked up to find his head resting in the soft lap of the girl he'd followed, "there was someone who clouted me stone unconscious for hours."

He said this without rancor; his head was not at all clear—and for that matter he was still not quite sure why he was here at all. He understood the familiar names and words that this Harathar of Narzunor uttered; but they were as difficult for his mind to hold on to in its present state as the man's own name and designation was difficult not to confuse. Hazuthor?

No matter; for the girl bent over him now, kissed him, smiled. He smiled back; and she seemed to frown slightly at Harathar.

"We have to protect our comings and goings, my friend," said Harathar. "At another time, you might have been lucky to catch a spear in your back. We like to bring our choices out at *our* convenience and direction."

The Bowman said nothing, having lost track again.

The Arzun, the Free Men, were those who had fled Qurval—and the descendants of all those who had fled him for the past ten thousand years.

This, the Bowman was mildly astonished to find he grasped; and he listened more attentively.

"We and our fathers and our mothers and theirs before came from Ophni, and from Ank, and from all the New Lands between, caught over the tens of centuries by Qurval's spell-storms. We have not forgot our cities and our greatnesses in the New Lands, though cast ashore forever in this legendary land of desolation.

"Yet do not think that where we found desolation, there is desolation still. Beyond this forest, incautious Bowman, there are more low hills, and other land for a number of days' march; and beyond that are the Five Cities of Narzunor.

"We founded them, we builded them, each of a different hue of stone, each drawn from separate quarries of a great shattered chain of mountains some fifty leagues to the east. These cities are splendid beyond my way with words. And safely we keep to ourselves in the land of Narzunor beyond our cities, making no unwise attempts at commerce through the high seas old-homeward to the New Lands, no, no! For Qurval's spells are oceanic; harmless to detect or affright us on land, they would be our ruin on broad Ocean.

"Since wise men as well as brave—and craven— have been caught out under the breath of the spell-storm, we have gained some store of wisdom, and, indeed, of power. Thus we offer sights you ne'er could dream to see elsewhere; having kept our children few, we have only our five cities to adorn.

"Trazmedorne of the pale golden marble; Fell'narai the Black, glistening night and day all in marble of ebon hue; Wzanarre, of rubystone from Older Karush-tun; Galnian the White of purest marble anywhere; and Dzabta . . . all of rainbow crystal, the which has ne'er been seen by any save the Arzun. For we dis-covered, virgin and solitary, the rainbow crystal quar-ry under ancient legendary 'Bta. The rich omens— well, but this, good Bowman, is legendary Armassic's soil we stand on; and the legends spoke truly, and always of beauty.

"Nonetheless, Qurval is dimly aware there are men and women out here; and from time to time he sends out a troop of his servants to capture some strong young men, for whom he has devious methods of making them desire to enter his service. That is the press. It is one reason we are here—for if we were not, Qurval might grow alarmed, send troops farther. We do not wish him to know of Narzunor."

"No," agreed the Bowman; for he sat stunned, his

mind clear for the time, understanding fully the incredible import of what he was hearing—men had been living on the empty lands of Pazatar and Armassic, all along!

And many in the New Lands did not even believe Pazatar and Armassic remained above the waves of Ocean!

At this the Bowman attempted dizzily to rise, and with a lurch he was on his feet. "Then you must be willing to fight!"

"Not necessarily," said Harathar. "Some might, however. We shall presently see; I have sent word round you may be leading a small force back to Daur'-umur."

"You have, eh?" said the Bowman, his face clouding. His head began to ache violently. "I'd like to see the man come that fetched me this clout. Stout arm."

The girl frowned, but Harathar grinned and slapped her on the shoulder. "Why, it was Ferieffa herself who served you, telling me she hadn't known she was followed till the moment she left the tunnel herself. Had she realized it was you in time to halt her blow, I doubt you would now hurt so!"

For the girl Ferieffa was moaning slightly in sympathy with the Bowman, and earnestly frowning in worry. "Well, lass," the Bowman said gruffly, "you have strength as well as skill."

Then he found strength to chuckle. "We will have a third fall, you and I, eh? After we've overthrown the wizard, freed his slaves, and—"

"I do not think you really believe this," said Harathar, dryly. "But you may leave when you wish, leading those who will go."

"*And* priceless information, at a guess on my character!" The Bowman shook his head in wonderment, and sighed. "I am dizzy. Now, what was I saying?"

And he fell forward and lay motionless.

A roll of thunder in the cloudless sky began trembling in the distance.

CHAPTER TEN:

A Game Of Ending

It was early afternoon without a cloud in the sky when thunder first began rolling over Daur'umur.

Then Qurval spoke throughout the palaces, and all paused. "There is always an exception."

The voice was heavy with inner satisfaction. "I have become weary of you all; and there is always a move which has precedence. Some among you know of it. It is called The Game Of Ending—and it is upon you *now*!"

There was a louder crash of thunder.

Konarr and Tassoran had been sitting at the window staring blankly down at variegated awning-colors; Laishalla was napping on a couch. As the Mad One's voice rang out and presently fell silent once more, they looked round at each other.

Brief echoes rang hollowly outside, and then there was a muttering of voices, puzzled to be halted in midst of their pleasures.

It was the fifth day of the Holiday Of The Nine Joys.

"Varnashoth spoke of it," said Laishalla, her voice chill and low as she now stood by them at the window. "The Game Of Ending—away with everyone in one last bacchanal of blood!" And she shuddered.

Sound of bronze-cleated boots in the outside hall;

the door splintered inward suddenly with a great crunch.

"Come along," a brownclad guard said from the doorway. He held a whip only, in his gloved hands; but he did not seem to expect to be disobeyed.

"The whip is daubed with herbs from 'kDuluoch, in Armassic," the guard said, moving the whip slightly; it glistened. "You will not know the lore, but it causes lingering, excruciating death—at a touch. Come along," he ended briskly.

They came; and others came, herded by Qurval's dismal brownrobed servants; each guard brandished whips.

Several men and women who had already dared the whips lay twisting and writhing in the courtyards as the gathering guests of Qurval passed through.

It was warning enough; and hence when all were finally herded together inside the great Hall of Feasting, and they found there were over a thousand of them and scarce a hundred of the servants in brown to guard the windows and exits, none thought to protest more than verbally.

"Is *that* all there were? Why, we could take them even now—*with* their whips!—if all would fight at a word!"

The man who spoke was tall and sturdy; and the markings on his houlder showed the innumerable lashings of a former galley-slave.

Changarth he was, who laughed always at the dangers of Daur'umur, or so I, Firanzu, later heard in fuller accompts than now I render you.

"Nay, you could not," said brownclad Hawkdeath, so named for the hooked sword with which he killed at Qurval's pleasure. He held his sword even now in one hand, while with the other he lazily switched the whip in a narrow arc.

"Could I not?" Changarth responded hotly, and drew himself unsteadily upward; for he was as nearly all were, still much-enhanced in mind by the joyful preparations Qurval had only now taken away from them.

"Nay," repeated Hawkdeath, raising the hooked point of his sword slightly, as the whip twitched on. "And not for the whips of 'kDuluoch alone! For now we take our leave of you forever, tiresome fools! And watch you afterwards through the hidden windows, and—" Hawkdeath had been laughing very like his mad master, when he was interrupted.

"*Nay!*" came Qurval's voice, sardonically imitating Hawkdeath's tone. "I watch you *all* now; there is no need for anyone to leave!"

The brown guards stood paralyzed; Laishalla pointed past one through a window.

"He's out there," she whispered to Konarr and Tassoran just behind her at the window. "In the Grahaln Tower; I've heard it in an old tale it was long-builded before the Autarchy was ever founded! Now this is important—you two have been enjoying the sweets of Qurval overmuch; he will have you taste the bitter now, if you—"

"Here I hold Eldest of Lightnings!" Qurval screamed. "None escape, none escape! Ha! Although they think they do! Those skin-clad fools skulking in the forests, they are done; they will be here by the time you are all quit of my game; then they shall unwilling help me to begin again! Ha-ha! It will be the nine hundred and twentyfourth Game Of Ending since the Great Fall! And the Great Fall of Pazatar and Armassic was ten thousand four hundred and thirtytwo years ago!"

Thunder rolled and rolled and rolled again across the blue and empty sky.

"Varnashoth told me also while you pleasured," Laishalla began whispering again as soon as she could be heard, "that when Qurval is here in Daur'umur, he spends most of his time in the Grahaln Tower. But Fain'umur is where most of his talismans of power, his great schemas, and his loreworks and volumes of deep magic are kept. Seldom does he bring one here of any power, and never more than one. Eldest of Lightnings! Powerful indeed!

"And if I could but find Varnashoth in this press and multitude," she went on, her voice by now normal as she looked distractedly about the huddled crowds of fearful prisoners, "perchance he'd know a way to scale the smooth sides of yon tower, four full stories; one might take the 'larrus in his cagelet, and bind him up for chops!"

As she spoke the last word there came a bolt of lightning; it smashed at the southwestern corner of the Palace of Feasting to the accompaniment of a thunderclap almost within the great chamber itself.

Screams came from where the bolt struck; a small gap had been opened in the wall of the building. Plaster, thin cement, and several small boulders used in the wall tumbled onto a pile of rubble that had buried some half a dozen.

Now Konarr jabbed Tassoran urgently with his elbow. "Pay attention! See, the guards! They tried to leave, and found their secret passages blocked with fresh dirt! What a groveling and howling!"

Tassoran grinned foolishly at Konarr and watched while several dozen guards were taken in their sad surprise by prisoners who had some particular revenge to take; until the remaining greyrobed figures took notice and formed together a circle, after which they were no longer attacked for fear of the whips of 'kDuluoch.

"Begins your final fall!" howled Qurval; and a series of flashes and booms ensued.

There were muffled, distant sounds of sundered masonry; and then at last someone screamed, "The roof! He's breaking through the roof of the palace with his lightning! Oriada! We shall be buried alive under it all!"

Dust was beginning to sift down through new cracks in the ceiling of the main hall. There were two more unused floors above, Konarr knew.

He shook Tassoran again, but the lad only grinned and said, "He must find it costly to destroy a whole palace just to kill a few people."

"What are you grinning about, you fool!" Konarr snapped irritatedly.

"Why, nothing," said Tassoran. "But I have had a kind of minor realization, lately; perhaps a day ago; it's all confusing. The wise ones teach of reincarnation, do they not? Well, I have seen the truth of it, or a taste; and hence poor Qurval can no longer worry me!"

"Damn the useless consolations of a too-late conversion!" Konarr shouted, his voice trembling with rage. "We must find a way out of this, for Laishalla at least."

"And what says Laishalla?" Tassoran said languidly.

Laishalla was staring intently out the window. "Look," she said, "how some have broken through the windows and are running by the dozens, scatteredly across yon courtyard."

Even as they looked there came a frightening crack; and a myriad tiny spears of lightning filled the courtyard for a moment.

This time the thunder was as the pounding of heavy hail, rather than the volcanic explosion of a mountainpeak.

And more than thirty bodies, half of them clad in brown, lay motionless in the courtyard.

"Well," said Tassoran, "perhaps we shouldn't leave *just* yet."

The Bowman groaned as he awoke.

"Good," said Harathar. "It was only a momentary dizziness, less than ten minutes. Your men have begun gathering."

The Bowman rose and staggered through the low door of the simple hut he had been lying inside. Several dozen young men of Narzunor stood there, with more coming in from the distance.

And each carried a bow, the smallest more than half the Bowman's height, the tallest to his shoulders.

"There is nothing like the bow," said Harathar. "Perhaps it is the real reason we trusted you."

"A good bow is an argument with many points!" said the Bowman. His father had once said that, before doom had fallen on them all; and the Bowman felt obscurely that it went well. It was at times like these he almost understood those folk who so bemused him by talking for hours at an end.

He shook his head to clear it of countless tag-ends of thoughts.

"You would be best to hurry, for everything our spies have said indicates Qurval's patience has grown thin," said Harathar. "These men are willing to join you; it is the first time we have struck directly against him."

"Wise men," said the Bowman suddenly, his full wits coming back to him for a time. "I'll warrant you're doing this for that Spellmaster, Varnashoth. *He* would have wisdom for you."

Harathar cocked his head at the Bowman. "Yes," he

said after a moment. "We have only recently discovered who this Varnashoth really is; and we want him. It might even happen that he wants us."

It was the Bowman's turn to cock his head, but he said nothing; for a man stood by him now, offering him a bow as tall as the Bowman's shoulders.

He strung it effortlessly, then nocked and let fly an arrow. It struck a wooden post thirty paces away, a hand'sbreadth above the daub of paint he'd taken for a mark.

"A trifle high," he said, without dissatisfaction. "With this I should have a hundredlength of good rope, and as much more good light twine; and mind you, fix the twine to a well-crafted arrow that is the heaviest you can find." This he spoke to the man who handed him the bow. "Bow isn't just a weapon; it's transportation, when you need it." He chuckled. "Who will guide us back to Daur'umur?"

"*I* shall!" Ferieffa announced, grinning impudently at the quick dour expression on the Bowman's face. "We have a third fall coming when the day is done!"

There were a few chuckles from behind the Bowman. "Very well," he said calmly, "lead us there, and quickly. And you and I, we shall ... fight it out later?"

His expression did not change; but she grinned at him.

"Very well," she said, mimicking him, "follow!" And she strode away immediately; the Bowman followed, and fortytwo Arzun; and disappeared into the bright-leaved forest.

They heard thunder again from the moment each dropped down into the little blank room and moved swiftly out into the corridor under Daur'umur.

"Faster," said the Bowman urgently as the thunder came again; and again; and again; and now they were running up two, three flights of stairs to the surface; and then they were at the front portals of the Palace of Wines (wherein those who tried to escape Qurval through drink could risk poison in any one of a hundred thousand rare flasks and vials in his cellars).

Where they now stood, they saw the Grahaln Tower just to their right, looming five smoothwalled stories up to great out-jutting stanchions that seemed to support some great invisible roof with purple magics glowing underneath. "Qurval," said Ferieffa unnecessarily.

In front of the Palace of Wines was a courtyard at the far side of which was the sorely battered Palace of Feasting; and at that moment came the thirty fleeing, and then atop of them the myriad spears of lightning; then silence and smell of burned flesh.

Laughter rang wildly through the deserted palaces of Daur'umur; and in the background were strains of indefinable mad music.

"So they all go, all, all, while even now my new servants approach!" Qurval's voice shouted unsteadily, after a great deal of laughter. "They shall see how great I am, and how puny all others! None can withstand the lightnings of B'kila S'foru, none save I! For B'kilu strikes in rare joy with me this day!"

A single bolt came down from the now-darkened cloudless sky of afternoon, and struck the Grahaln Tower right at its peak; but the great invisible roof glowed somewhat, and all knew Qurval was safe.

The Grahaln Tower was unmarked; and then a lesser bolt struck the Palace of Feasting, knocking down another portion of façade from the upper stories to the accompaniment of screams from inside.

"Scream on!" howled Qurval. "Your dark moment has come when you shall be driven down, down, past degradations of fear in this life and in endless ones to come, for I hold the Key! Seek it elsewhere, that Key!"

The manic voice broke often, now, to gasp for breath, so loudly was Qurval calling into his mystic device.

"Seek it, perchance, the *next* time you find yourselves drawn to this doomed shore! As so many of you have been before, *so many times!*" (And Konarr said, "I do not believe him," but Tassoran's face was sudden-struck with doubtful fear.)

At regular intervals now the lightning bolt struck; and only part of the second floor was left.

The Bowman had made up his mind and was already at the base of the Grahaln Tower. "He will be looking only to the Palace of Feasting, I'm certain," he said to Ferieffa as she and the rest came up around him again.

"He has no reason to suppose we threaten him," said Ferieffa. "He thinks we are drawn here by his men and spells, and pays no attention to us."

"He *knows* we stand here?"

"Would you have come, had you realized this before?"

"No," said the Bowman, but he was grinning; for one of the Arzun handed him now a heavy arrow, to which was attached a light line.

For a moment the Bowman frowned at the arrow itself, as if he had once more forgotten just what he was about; then he shook his head and looked upward, almost absent-mindedly stringing his bow.

He marked his target in the glare of a bolt of lightning. "Were this a true storm," he chuckled suddenly, "the wind would make this impossible. Magic too has its disadvantages."

The next flash found him ready, and in the brief moment of fullest light he let fly at one of the tower's roof-stanchions.

The glare of the next bolt showed the arrow falling short. Quickly the arrow was brought back to the Bowman, and he let fly again at the next light.

This time the arrow fell over the projecting bar of smooth metal before it curved upward to support the roof; and the heavy arrow began to pull the light line over the stanchion.

But now the lad holding the line was tugging futilely.

The Bowman gave it several sharp tugs, and the line began paying out again; a moment later the arrow fell to the hardpacked soil.

Frantically the climbing-rope was knotted into the line, and hauled up over the stanchion. Finally the two ends of the rope were secured for climbing, and the Bowman immediately began to haul himself up, strung bow hung over his right shoulder, arrows tight-packed in the quiver.

And for many long breaths they watched while intermittant flashes in the now almost-complete darkness picked out the Bowman, steadily clambering upward while behind him the Palace of Feasting took bolt after bolt of lightning.

CHAPTER ELEVEN:

Eyes Of The Eldest

The Bowman peered cautiously over the stanchion before hauling himself up over the edge of the roof-platform.

There stood the tall, thin figure of Qurval, the Wizard of Storms, amid a demon's den of magical devices the Bowman found it hard to look at.

In his hands Qurval held a strange jewel big as three hens' eggs; it was shifting-colored, smooth, and subtly curved—until at closer look the Bowman thought it scarred and pitted fearfully even while it glowed with pure colors as though surfaced of smoothest finish.

Qurval stared at the jewel for a time, then looked into a great cloud of green smoke that hovered to his left. Moments later there came a lightning bolt just behind the Bowman, or so it felt; the Palace of Feasting had taken another blow. Somehow it was managed through the green smoke, the Bowman knew; and he came over the rail while the Wizard's glance was elsewhere.

Now huddled behind a large jar, from which came a rich indefinable aroma, the Bowman looked closer at the green cloud—and saw the unmistakable ruined outlines of the Palace of Feasting, a part of the side wall now completely shattered away. He looked behind him, and saw that the palace itself lay in the same sad broken condition.

And now Qurval was beginning to aim his bolts for the open part of the wall, slaughtering by the dozens with each blow. The Bowman watched intently, arrow nocked and ready; then Qurval held the jewel more carelessly, studying dim figures in his conjured smoke.

The Bowman let fly; with a howl of pain Qurval staggered back, clutching one bleeding hand with one whole one.

And Eldest of Lightnings bounced sluggishly several times on the black marble paves, then rolled on toward a tall empty cabinet ... or was there a faint blue mist inside?

The Bowman ran forward with all his speed, and was only moments from the jewel when Qurval saw him—too late to prevent it!

Then the Bowman reached the jewel, touched it gingerly, picked it up; it was warm, but not hot.

"Fool!" said Qurval in triumphant low tones. "Would you so casually handle B'kila S'foru, Eldest of Lightnings himself from the great works before the beginning of time?" And Qurval laughed, quietly ... and horribly.

The Bowman looked doubtfully at the jewel for a moment. Scarred, pitted, yet pure, with a central luminous core that—

The Bowman staggered, dropping the jewel. It rang dully on the polished black stone as he strained painfully for breath; there had been a surge of unutterable power; he had been unable to bear it.

The jewel was free again!

He leaped for it along with Qurval's lunge, and they collided heavily and fell both to the floor.

Once more Eldest of Lightnings rolled slowly to the

cabinet of blue mist, while Qurval attempted to get to his knees for another desperate lunge. But the Bowman threw himself again at Qurval, knocking him halfway into the misty cabinet.

For a brief time the Wizard of Storms lay panting, and the Bowman got wearily to his feet once more.

His head had now been cracked twice against the flagstones; it burned almost unbearably. It was much the same, the day after he had drunk the smallkeg of ale on the day of his majority; at eleven, that was, for life was swiftly hard in the ancient hills of The 'Derh south of Ank and Oan.

"Enough of this," said Qurval as he lay panting; his voice shook. "I have not been soiled by physical violence in over a thousand years! I choose to endure *no more!*"

The Wizard quickly reached for Eldest of Lightnings as it lay by his feet; then kicked himself sprawling backward into the cabinet.

But at the same time the Bowman lurched forward, and was falling heavily beside him in the cabinet. . . .

"Curse you!" said the Wizard bitterly. "I didn't mean to bring you along *here!* Well, you are rarely privileged, fool, most rarely privileged!"

It seemed they lay in the same cabinet—yet the room they were in bore little resemblance to the top of the tower called Grahaln. For one wall seemed a sheet of purest unmarked gold; another was black, with a blaze of diamond-sparkling lights; another wall roared silently in endless flaming streams upward, though the room was not warm; but the last wall he did not see, for Qurval had made as if to dart from the cabinet.

The Bowman slashed an arm outward, staggering Qurval; then they both got slowly to their feet.

But now one giant hand held the talisman of B'kila

S'foru; and with the other, the Bowman hit Qurval again.

Qurval screamed with incoherent rage and made a great sweeping gesture, uttering at the same time an incomprehensible word of power—and the Bowman dropped to the ground as if hit by one of the white marble pavingstones.

When Tassoran caught sight of the Bowman, almost up to the top of the Grahaln Tower, he gave a shout, and the others saw. Then, the Bowman was over the top, loosing an arrow inside the tower ... and when no lightnings came after some moments, Tassoran spoke decisively.

"This is a foolish death, to wait for stone walls to crumble in, exposing us to lightnings from the dark cloudless sky! I say the Bowman has distracted Qurval; this may be our only chance to escape his games at last!".

Konarr grinned and slapped Tassoran on the back; and then the two and Laishalla were out of a burned window and running across the courtyard at the tower, followed by an ever-increasing horde from the Palace of Feasting.

When he reached the dangling rope, Tassoran took hold of the loose ends and, without asking leave, began climbing; and Laishalla was directly behind him. On the ground, Konarr was caught momentarily in an argument.

When Tassoran's head peered up over the stanchion, the top of the Grahaln Tower was empty! He hauled himself over the edge and rested a moment, gasping for breath, as Laishalla came up over, also breathing hard.

Tassoran came to his feet, and Konarr joined them.

"We are in mystery," said Tassoran. "Neither the Bowman nor Qurval are here!"

They moved on past the jar of sweetsmelling herbs ("Seldomgrass," said Laishalla) and looked round the empty platform.

Then Laishalla swerved and looked more closely at the cabinet of blue mist; and a look of triumph came over her face.

Within the blue mist could still be seen the shadowy outlines of two forms—"Qurval and the Bowman as they were when they departed!" she said aloud, and the other two looked back at her in puzzlement from where they stood by the green smoky image of the Palace of Feasting. In the smoke they could see people still fleeing the building, though the lightnings had ceased with the Bowman's last shot.

But now it was Laishalla's turn to look blankly past them, for the great green cloud shivered convulsively—and began reforming into a head—a cowled head!

"Fortune guides us," came a sardonic voice familiar to Tassoran; and he looked round for a weapon.

Over the edge of the roof now were coming men with bows at the ready; he asked for one, nocked an arrow, and aimed for the green smoke.

"For," the voice was saying, "the careless Qurval is working in seldomsmoke, and I can reach it. You there," and the face of Taher Kmatis appeared as the figure in the seldomsmoke threw back his cowl and seemed to peer outward. "Konarr, are you there?"

"*I* am here, filth," said Tassoran hotly, and raised the bow. "And I shall send an arrow through—"

"Through my simulacrum there, oh, yes," said Taher Kmatis, grinning. "Please do, poor idiot. It would hurt me so much."

Tassoran loosed the shaft without thinking. It tore

through the insubstantial smoke and shattered against a stone pillar behind it.

Apart from wavering for a moment, the face of Taher Kmatis remained.

"Loss of a good arrow," said Konarr by Tassoran's side, and Tassoran suppressed a sudden almost overwhelming urge to reach out and fetch the Captain a sound blow over the ear.

Taher Kmatis' shadowface chuckled. "I take it you followed my suggestion; you were always easy to dupe. Now, Konarr: I counsel you to forget the past. To remember is always to remember ills done one; and that is mere self-injury. Enough; I take it Qurval has fled to another point of safety?"

"He has," said Konarr irritably. "Get on, then; I have heard something of you, ser Spellmaster Taher, and deeds you've done in Kazemi and elsewhere. Yet I'll listen."

"Lies and truth intermixed is all you've heard, good Captain, said Taher Kmatis calmly. "Well; and are any of Qurval's talismans lying about, perchance? I would rather expect not, but you might look."

"How would we know his talismans?" muttered Tassoran, while the Arzun began looking around at random, having no better idea than Tassoran did.

"Eldest of Lightnings, he has," mused Taher. "That is a fine one, though getting weaker with great age as I think now; for he must have been using it moments before I made clear contact. It was very strong in the upper registers of ... well, but surely he has it with him wherever he's gone. We must plan some other means of—"

"What could we do if we had the talisman of B'kila S'foru?" asked Laishalla suddenly.

"Why, stare into it, lass, whoever you are; and when you see aught looking back, look to the spot you wish his lightning to strike, or at a replication of it properly supported. Eldest of Lightnings will make his gigantic stroke once more, at your bidding. But, you must be strong of will, and full of courage; or you cannot control B'kila S'foru, or his bolts where they may fall!"

"Well," began Tassoran; but without another word Laishalla darted for the cabinet of blue mist, was inside—

—and disappeared.

The Bowman lay crumpled at Qurval's feet as Laishalla stepped silently out of the cabinet behind the tall old madman.

Qurval kicked petulantly at the Bowman's leg, kicked it again, then leaned down and cuffed him severely in the face, drawing blood.

The Bowman shook his head, and very slowly began once more to get to his feet.

At that moment Laishalla saw the pulsating brilliant jewel that was Eldest of Lightnings.

It lay on the white marble flagstones, back behind Qurval. Hardly a moment later she had it in her hands, and holding its cool smoothness up, she stared into it.

"*No!*" howled Qurval as he turned to see Laishalla confronting Eldest of Lightnings. But before he could take a step toward her—

—she saw forms swirling in innumerable colors at the inner life of the jewel; then

—*eyes*, B'kila S'foru's *eyes;* old, said legend, when time began for Pazatar and Armassic; B'kila S'foru, Eldest of Lightning, whose essence, locked somehow in the incredible crystal, now peered back into her own eyes, and Laishalla remembered now patches of

her life long forgotten, and she stared more deter-
minedly at the *eyes* as they seemed to bore down
through her last inner defenses, the ones she herself
never tried to crack, to learn about herself, and then
impossibly the *eyes* were drawn away now, but
seemed charged with power, and *look where you
wish the bolt to strike,* something inside her said, and

—she turned and looked full at Qurval, Wizard of
Storms, and Qurval moved his lips desperately without saying anything, and a gigantic flash of lightning
instantly followed by an incredible thundering boom
thudded insensately, batteringly, through the chamber. . . .

The great hot glow of lightning seemed to surround
Qurval; he stood against it till it winked away, writhing as he still attempted to speak.

Then as afterlight died away and ears could hear
other sounds, Qurval slumped over slowly to his knees
in a twisting fall, then limply tumbled over onto his
side.

CHAPTER TWELVE:

Further Conversations Of An Immortal

There was a muffled explosion somewhere within the walls of Daur'umur. The Arzun and those prisoners well enough were firing as many of the Wizard of Storm's secret passages, torture rooms, observation rooms, and other installations as they could find.

"Glad to hear your comrades are making good use of their time." Zantain's visage in the seldomsmoke was still drawn with pain, but his voice was cheerful. "There is no way to know how long Qurval will remain as he is from the effects of the lightning."

"We have found a number of objects that may be instruments of greater or lesser power; which you will need to see," said Konarr.

"You won't have much more time to look," said Zantain. "Can you tell the use of any of these objects?"

"First, we hold Eldest of Lightnings now, or rather Laishalla does," said Tassoran.

"B'kila S'foru has made it clear that he wishes only me to channel his power, while in his present service," she said, rather diffidently.

"Second, we have located books of power, which none of us can read. Laishalla nearly was killed when she touched one." Tassoran did not show outwardly how this had shaken him.

Zantain nodded in the green smoke.

"Third, the Arzun now have two of Qurval's five Stones of Protection, the one called Vidaisha and the one called Vuldirian. He was not wearing these two, since they interfered with B'kila S'foru. As for the three he wears, we cannot of course obtain them. Vuldushur. Vedara protected him during sexual con- but his downfall was in the other two, Vedara and Vuldushur. Vedara protected him during sexual congress and as a consequence had been infrequently used in the past several millennia, or so said Varnashoth; so that as a result Vedara had grown sleepy and careless and frequently beguiled the attention of the guardian Vuldushur. Now, Vuldushur was supposed to protect Qurval while his attention was distracted; but alas for Qurval, it was Vuldushur's attention that was distracted. . . ."

Tassoran paused. "This Varnashoth," he recollected, then, "assured us that Qurval would remain unconscious for two full days. Therefore we shall be safe if we spend but the one here."

Laishalla now spoke. "I used Eldest of Lightnings against his platform of great schemas in Fain'umur, thoroughly enough so that he will not be calling spellstorms for several fiftydays, perhaps even years. He may well be a target for sea-rovers, once word is current of this day. But they'd better be quick, for the old snake will grow a magic new skin!"

"Do you think you will find any more points of power?" Zantain asked.

"No," said Tassoran. "There are skulking servants in Fain'umur that did not face his doom but stayed to serve him; these keep almost out of sight, though they are hiding what they can practically under our feet. And they have the advantage, knowing what is truly valuable and where it is."

Zantain sighed. "Well, Eldest of Lightnings is no

small prize. Tell me, will the one you call the Bowman return with you here? I would have to meet him,
but it may be he shall be called to join us."

"Nay," said the Bowman, climbing up onto the
platform atop the Grahaln Tower. He turned and
helped an old man in grey robes.

It was Varnashoth the Eld, Spellmaster of Sezain.

"I have been speaking of my adventures to this
wise man," said the Bowman, "and finally he has
recalled that I am one he put a geas on, years before.
Under this geas, of course, I surely may not join you."

Varnashoth nodded in agreement. "I am afraid not.
Your high service, Master Zantain, immortal though
you say you are, cannot supervene in geas-bindings
imposed by a Spellmaster of my degree. Not I, but
the geas binds him now, alas, or perhaps I would
yield you my reluctant hero.

"Only when Miethnara, the kiula of Jeshne, is freed
from conquest-bondage to whomever holds her captive now, will the Bowman be freed. And then, let me
add, only if having slain her captor he sets her free
unmolested. Not easy, that last; for Miethnara is fair
indeed, and of a spirit to ensorcel any man's unwilling
soul!"

Tassoran stood with jaw agape. "But—the kiula of
Jeshne! Ilnivar! Ilnivar held her, in 's tiny prison! No
ransom accepted, ran the story in the market. And
the Bowman *slew* Ilnivar!"

The Bowman looked at Varnashoth, who looked
mildly back and said, "Then, perhaps you have
fulfilled your geas already."

"*That* is why I was permitted to do the deed in the
first place!" said the Bowman, and for the first time
they saw his face grin broadly. "And permitted to
come along with Tassoran and these others into some
other—"

"Some other mythos, yes," said Varnashoth, and his tone was dry. "It is true that I might have made further use of you myself, but here you have found four stalwart comrades to go off adventuring with! It would not serve my style of purposes to prevent you from that!"

"Yet," said the Bowman, "I have no desire to go off adventuring, alone or with good comrades. I wish to find my own bow somewhere in this cursed warren of evil, and to return to The 'Derh, my geas done. Little enough awaits me in the hills, but it is all I—"

"No, once more," said Varnashoth, now stern. "Your fate long since was separated from that of The 'Derh, and all those who lived there; this I can tell you from my wisdom.

"So, go with these others; there you will find that which no wise man is wise enough to speak of: your true fate, call it."

"Portentious, but—" the Bowman started to say, shaking his head.

"*Four* comrades?" asked Tassoran suddenly.

"There is the girl," said Zantain from the seldomsmoke, quietly. "She too is fit to be a hero."

Laishalla's fair skin turned paler. "I ... I am a wanderer," she said at last. "I have that in my past which is not in the past of heroes."

"And she is only a woman!" said Tassoran, then paused and flushed in confusion. "That is ... I mean. . . ."

"What are heroes?" said Konarr suddenly. "Are *we* heroes? Tassoran, former thief; Konarr, former sailor, former Captain—"

"You are the people," I said, stepping forth beside Zantain that I might be seen in the seldomsmoke, "that scribes and, yes, legendtellers such as myself speak of in our tales of great mysterious events. And thus you are heroes."

I greatly dared in this, being only Firanzu of Mallion and—certes!—no hero myself. "You are heroes for you partake in the doing of great deeds. See, then, Item firstly: thief and Captain steal talismans of great-feared power from the Lady Tza—preventing her from sorely wracking the half our entire world, in her idle and misunderstanding experimentations. Item secondly, you have put down a great scourge and fiend of Ocean; albeit only for a brief time. Item thirdly, by thus you have freed many prisoners who else would wretchedly have perished. Item fourthly, you are the means direct whereby the peaceful Arzun may maintain themselves in greater security. And then there are other Items that even legend-tellers do not bother much with telling of; we'd all soon tire of hearing."

"Soon, indeed, Master Firanzu," said Zantain, dryly sarcastic, and he placed a hand on my shoulder; it pinched not gently.

"Still, old Captain," said Tassoran, turning to Konarr, "isn't it—in a way—for the tales they'd tell if they but knew, that we've gone off with ser Zantain? Master," he said, now facing Zantain with a grin, "the legendteller speaks truly."

"If he has persuaded you, then he is free," said Zantain, and took his hand from my shoulder; but it ached for days thereafter. "Firanzu, go and speak truth always." Again that sardonic tone.

"As always," I returned, and bowed deeply; it was the bow sarcastic of the courts of the Lady Tza, and it seemed me ser Zantain took my meaning clear enough.

"Items two of the truth," I dared to go on, as I tried to ease my shoulder. "Firstly, you should not have freed this spellmastering skulker called Kmatis."

"Taher again?" said Varnashoth. "He persists in folly."

Zantain answered. "He helped me in my time of trouble—which yet continues, good Konarr, and requires you hasten with the Cup of Tron. I did not wish deep offense and troubles to us all by confronting two brothers so far in enmity."

Said Tassoran, bitterly, "Once there were *three* brothers—you might ask Taher about the middle one, some day when you join again in alliance with him."

"You are perhaps justly offended," said Zantain. "But I had no other man to use, when he presented himself unknowingly."

"Secondly of the truth," I continued, "you have forgot the great ship that bore you to this land; I was here; I heard you speak of it to Zantain." This I addressed to them generally, though they seemed disposed enough to completely ignore me; then, done, I stepped back from the seldomsmoke.

"True," Konarr admitted, "and a fine ship it was, too. If this scrying-smoke could be tuned to it, we might find it worthwhile to make the tedious journey there."

"It would be a question of the Wizard of Storms," said Zantain. "And I do not think that he will be free to search for your lone ship, for quite some time after he regains his senses. There will be too many things for him to look to, by far."

"Then let us take the ship!" Tassoran said. "For it is splendid!"

Laishallà stepped forward, eyes shining. "I do not really know what sort of fellowship this is, my friends, that you make such general and open conversation about it. Still, to have a ship that's built in Teriathna is no small advantage; and if we do not find Lord Raganas too quickly, why, the *Ahthrthu* is ours to—"

"We would have to find Lord Raganas, I think," said Zantain. "But perhaps he will be happy enough just to find his private treasure-chambers unentered— if Qurval's brown minions have not already plundered it. From what you said, Raganas holds there enough of value to buy twenty *Ahthrthus*."

"And we take the ship itself for salvage," said Konarr. "Give him his treasure in fairness; that would do it nicely! We'll try it! It's a fair ship indeed!"

"Salvage!" the Bowman snorted. "Were it not for us, the *Ahthrthu* would be plying the coasts of the New Lands this moment!"

"We could take a ship from here," said Laishalla. "There are enough seaworthy vessels here to take all back across Ocean; while we sail to the *Ahthrthu*. Thus if it has been hulled by waves and rocks or sunk by guards, we may sail directly away in safety."

"Enough of this all!" said Zantain. "You have much to do, no matter what your decisions. You have many hours left to do Qurval's future plans great damage."

"Well," said Tassoran, "I suppose so."

He looked around and all nodded assent.

Zantain nodded then; and presently his face disappeared in a bright green spray. . . .

"Well," said Tassoran again, this time more to Konarr in particular, "I suppose we've just been through our second adventure."

"We *all* have been through our *first* adventure, together," said Konarr. "But no matter the past; for the present ends in a very prosaic episode. For we have much to do in demolishing Qurval's works."

"There should be trumpets!" said Tassoran. Yet he was laughing at the idea as he spoke. "Instead, why, we're ending in the middle of a conversation!"

"No," said the Bowman, "it ends in simple work. That is enough; for that is the way of all life."

"Work now," said Laishalla, mischief-smiling, "but it will not end that way. Don't you know? There's always more."

—end of
The Ninth Scroll of Firanzu

★ ★ Belmont Specials ★ ★

Special offer on these books below—Two 60c books for $1.00. Two 75c books for $1.25. The following books are not included in the 5 for 4 book offer, but we invite you to take advantage of the special price.

☐ **THE YOKE AND THE STAR,** by Tana de Gámez
A beautiful bawdy novel by the author of the sensational best seller LIKE A RIVER OF LIONS. A widely acclaimed, explosively adult novel about the inflamed passions of love and the fierce betrayals of war.   #B95-106, 95¢

☐ **SEX FUN AND GAMES,** by Ruy Traube
An intimate guidebook for married couples.   #B95-107, 95¢

☐ **VENUS IN FURS,** by Leopold Sacher-Masoch
The famous underground masterpiece of sexual aberration that shook the world of erotica.   #B75-220, 75¢

☐ **SWING HIGH SWEET PUSSYCAT,** by D. Royal
A probing psychosexual report of a modern day problem—when is a girl too young?   #B75-219, 75¢

☐ **COOL KIDS WITH HOT IDEAS,** by Jules Archer
A probing case history report of young girls in trouble.   #B75-221, 75¢

☐ **THE X REPORT,** selections from Sexology Magazine
A survey by leading doctors of modern sex patterns and practices among men and women of all ages.   #B75-222, 50¢

☐ **THE LUSTS OF CASANOVA,** by Jacques Casanova
The most riotous, ribald memoirs of the world's most notorious lover.
        #B75-223, 75¢

☐ **CONFESSIONS OF A RAKE**—Anonymous
The erotic education of a young Victorian debaucher.   #B12-1007, $1.25

☐ **HEAT,** by John O'Mara
Two men and a woman—bound together by money lust. One was naive . . . it wasn't the woman.   #B60-1009, 60¢

☐ **THE SOFA,** by Crebillon Fils
Memoirs of scandal and strange desire.   #B95-108, 95¢

☐ **FOR MEN ONLY,** by Beth Brown
The flamboyant best-seller about "The Oldest Profession."   #B60-088, 60¢

NON-FICTION

☐ **FLYING SAUCERS: HOAX OR REALITY?,** by L. Jerome Stanton
This is a common sense, technically accurate report on UFOs, offering the first sound approach to the questions: What are they? From where do they come? Is extrastellar intelligent life possible? Are we in danger?   #B50-761, 50¢

☐ **WORLD OF THE WEIRD,** by Brad Steiger
Startling, astounding, shocking . . . but incredibly true! A collection of stories of human beings, and animals who defy all known laws of science and nature.
        #B50-727, 50¢

☐ **DISCOVER FLYING,** by Robert Scharff
(Orig. title: WHO, ME FLY?)
If you can drive a car you can discover flying . . . and if you can afford a car you can own a plane. Here's what it takes to learn how to fly—and broaden your pleasure horizons.   #B75-1014, 75¢

GOTHIC SUSPENSE NOVELS

☐ **BRIDE OF DEATH,** by Mary Reisner
The tragedy of Morestone Manor had destroyed many lives—now Stella feared she too would be a BRIDE OF DEATH.   #B50-807, 50¢

☐ **DEATH HALL,** by Mary Reisner
Her sunlit dream of love and happiness was torn apart by a scream of fear.
        #B60-072, 60¢

☐ **THE SECRET OF DRESDEN FARM,** by Genevieve St. John
Myra Linden came to Gregory Mansion to unravel a twenty-five-year-old secret. And the only person who could help her was a murderer.   #B50-832, 50¢

☐ **BLUE DEVIL SUITE,** by Dorothy Daniels
Ghosts that kill; rumors that terrify—but only Peggy believed the danger to be real.   #B50-838, 50¢

BELMONT'S BEST
in
Swords & Sorcery

B50-863	**GIANT OF WORLD'S END** Lin Carter	50¢
B50-849	**WHOM THE GODS WOULD SLAY** Ivar Jorgensen	50¢
B50-809	**THE THIEF OF THOTH** Lin Carter **AND OTHERS SHALL BE BORN** Frank Belknap Long (A Belmont Double Novel)	50¢
B50-804	**TOWER AT THE EDGE OF TIME** Lin Carter	50¢
B50-759	**FLAME OF IRIDAR** Lin Carter **PERIL OF THE STARMEN** Kris Neville (A Belmont Double Novel)	50¢
B50-751	**THE JEWELS OF ELSEWHEN** Ted White	50¢
